No One Needed to Know

D1304263

D. G. Driver

<u>Other novels by D. G. Driver</u>

The Juniper Sawfeather Novels
Cry of the Sea
Whisper of the Woods
Echo of the Cliffs

Passing Notes

For my family, especially Joe

Re-tard /riˈtärd/ verb. To slow the progress of: delay.
*Webster's Dictionary

Ri-tard /rihˈtärd/ verb. A shortened version of the word *ritardando*, which is a term used in **music** to refer to gradually becoming slower.
*www.yourdictionary.com/ritard

In 2012, the federal government enacted legislation changing the term **mental retardation** to **intellectual disabilities** in all federal law. Despite being encouraged to quickly replace all references to mental retardation and its derivatives, some state offices have still not made the changes to the less offensive term in their legislation and documents.
*http://www.specialeducationguide.com/disability-profiles/intellectual-disability/

Retard is <u>not</u> a noun.

Retard is <u>not</u> a name.

Table of Contents

It's Always "No"   1
Bullies   9
The Girls   13
Friday After   21
The Notes   29
My Turn to be Mean   35
At the Movies   43
Nowhere to Go   51
A Teenage Makeover   58
Not Like My Brother   65
Hiding   71
At the Dance   78
A Surprising Night   85
Monday Morning   96
What It's Like to be Special   106
Teaching and Learning   114
Someone Gets it Right   122
Yes   125
Author's Note and Resources   127

1

It's Always "No"

"I see the mad bomber off the port bow!"

I cupped my hands around my eyes as if they were binoculars to see my brother Donald, who stood gingerly in the creaky crow's nest. I called out to him, "Can you get an angle on him?"

"I think so," Donald shouted back. "Is he close?"

"Getting closer every second. Looks like he's going to ram us. Shoot him quick or brace for impact!"

Donald raised his arms to imitate holding an automatic rifle and fired off half a dozen shots. "Zhoo, zhoo, zhoo, zhoo, zhoo, zhoo!" He lowered his hands to get his balance again. "Did I get him, Heidi?"

"No," I answered. It was always no. I can't explain why my impulse was always to turn him down. His ideas never seemed good to me. Mine were always better. "You missed. Hold on tight."

Donald gripped the wood around him as tightly as he could. I ducked behind the rail of the ship and covered my head. "BAM!" I screamed as loud as I could. I jumped backwards and rolled over. Donald shook the crow's nest to make it look like the boat was breaking apart. He wasn't daring enough to try a stunt. Even if he did get the guts, he probably would have hurt himself. I guess he knew that.

"He got us good," I said, wheezing as though I were in a lot of pain. "I think we're going to sink."

"Climb up here," Donald suggested.

"No. You come down. Help me repair the hole." I limped back to the ship's railing. Donald slowly climbed down the ladder to the main deck. "Hurry up. Water's leaking."

"I'm going as fast as I can."

There were few things as awkward looking as Donald trying to walk across the deck as though it were a foot deep in water. I thought his long legs made him look like an ostrich. It was hard not to laugh at him, but I sucked it in. This wasn't the time. Instead, I wiped my forehead with the back of my arm like I'd seen my favorite action heroes do in the movies when they were working really hard. I could almost feel the seawater and grease dirtying my face. I imagined that I looked good, like a real action star with my bright blond, shoulder-length hair tied back in a ponytail and a red bandanna knotted around my neck. For the thousandth time I wished my parents hadn't named me Heidi. That was a name for a girl in braids and bonnets. Why couldn't they have named me Storm or Raven or Natasha or even Scarlett?

"I can't fix it," I sighed as dramatically as possible. "We're going to have to swim for it."

I lurched myself over the side of the boat and jumped into the sand surrounding it. Though on my feet, I stroked my arms to show that I was swimming away from the boat. After a short distance I stopped, faced the boat, and changed my hand movements to make it look as though I were treading water. My feet dug back and forth in the crunchy sand. "Come on, Donald! Jump!"

Donald climbed up on the railing of the ship. It was only a four-foot drop. It could hardly hurt him, especially since he was already five-foot-six. Still, he hesitated.

"Come on," I hollered. "You're going to drown!"

Donald looked back toward the stepladder on the side of the boat behind him that led to the sand. He inclined toward it.

"Don't take the ladder. That's for wimps. No time. Just jump!"

"I . . ." Donald looked at me and adjusted his glasses. He grinned in that funny way of his where his forehead stayed wrinkled as though he might cry. It was always strange for me to see Donald's face take on two expressions at the same time like that. I knew that it meant I was pushing him too hard. He would break down if I didn't let up. Not cry or blubber or anything like that. He'd just stop functioning. All

3

the decision-making parts of his brain would fizzle out. I'd have to lead him around like a pet dog.

But, my goodness, I thought. *It's only four feet.*

"Just jump already," I whined at him.

Donald lifted one of his skinny legs over the railing so that he was straddling it. Sitting on top of the railing made the fall seem higher. I knew that from experience, and I could see it all over his face. Only recently had I mastered the art of jumping off fences and short walls. It had been a long-time goal of mine. None of my other girlfriends could do it, but all the boys at school could. Now I could play tag the cool way, with a little danger—and with all the boys. Looking at my brother stuck up on that ship railing, I could tell he was majorly chickening out. Poor Donald. He'd never be able to play tag the cool way.

Donald crept his other leg over the railing and balanced on his stomach, his face leaning into the boat, his bottom jutting out toward me. He gripped the edge with his hands and slid his body down the side of the boat until his sneakers touched the sand. It was agonizing to watch him do this. Each movement took an eternity as he tried to figure out the process. Anyone else would have been down before Donald even got started.

At last, he let go of the boat, staggered backwards a step or two, and then turned around and pretended to swim toward me as though he had played the game without a hitch.

By this time I had stopped pretending to tread water. I crossed my arms and stood with my legs open so that most of my weight was on one foot.

"I can't believe how lame you are," I said to him.

4

Donald stopped "swimming." His hands fluttered about him as though he needed someone to tell him what to do with them. After a moment, he let his thumbs drift to the front pockets of his jeans. He never responded to me. I didn't expect him to. He had that typical look on his face that made people wonder whether he'd heard them or just didn't understand what they'd said. I figured Donald didn't know what he'd done to prompt me calling him lame.

"I don't feel like playing anymore," I said.

"Do you want to go to another park?" Donald asked. He turned his head and squinted into the sun.

"No," I replied. Since he wasn't looking, I turned my back to him. The guilt was less intense if I didn't see his face. "I want to go home. This is boring."

And it *was* boring. Not nearly as much fun as it used to be. Even though this was the only interesting playground left in our city in Southern California, it just didn't seem interesting enough anymore. For the past two years all the parks had been going through reconstruction. A bunch of mothers in the community felt the parks weren't safe enough. All cement castles, wooden forts, tall winding slides, teeter-totters, and merry-go-rounds had been trashed, replaced with bright orange and blue staircases and plastic slides.

This park, the only one of its kind left, had a life-sized boat stuck in a sandbox to look like a shipwreck. It was full of places to hide and climb—and probably spiders. I tried not to think about that too much when I played on it. Right next to it was this bizarre cement structure with tunnels to creep through. It looked like a flying saucer. Both were great for playing make-believe. The orange and blue "big toys" were not good at all for that kind of playing. Occasionally they might have a steering wheel randomly hitched to a protective railing, but what fun was that? Were we kids supposed to think we were driving a funky jungle gym through space? Driving it through the ocean?

Because this was the only park worth my time, I planned my weekends around playing there. It was a long bike ride from home. We had to take this bike path that connected three different subdivisions, pass by two different elementary schools, and cross a bridge that went over the train tracks to get there. So a considerable chunk of a Saturday afternoon had to be spent just getting there and back again. For a while I gave up Saturday morning cartoons so Donald and I could get going earlier. It was better to get to the park before the babies showed up.

When the park got too crowded, the two of us would head to the shopping center to get hamburgers before going home. Our house was in a subdivision set off the main road in town. Basically, it was a few blocks from our house to get to that street. We only had to cross through one light to get to the shopping center, so all the kids in my neighborhood biked or walked there. My mom was always telling me how our town kept growing bigger and bigger on the outside, but this little part in the middle stayed the same. That's why my parents bought a house there, not far from the house where my mom grew up. She liked the safety and convenience of it all.

I always liked having everything so close, too, because we had a lot more freedom in our neighborhood than kids in other areas. My mom felt pretty secure about letting us wander around without her, as long as we checked in regularly by phone. But going to the park didn't excite me like it used to. I found myself dreading the outing with Donald instead of looking forward to it. Cartoons were back in my life, and I often skipped the hamburger so I could get back home as soon as possible.

The problem was that I was starting to feel too old for pretending. I was in sixth grade, and none of the other girls at school were playing games where they became pirates, superheroes, or monsters. No one wanted to go through spaceship tunnels and convince each other that when they came out on the other end they would be on Mars. No one even wanted to play house or dolls anymore. Now it was all about who liked who and who was going to the mall to buy lipstick.

I mostly went on these park trips to entertain Donald. Unlike me, he wasn't outgrowing make-believe games. He was sixteen, but he seemed more like nine or ten. Maybe eight. True, he was starting to look his age. He was growing fast and had little wiry hairs on his chin. He had more pimples than the entire high school student body put together. But it was the way his dark hair always had that greasy look, even though he washed it every day, and how the thick glasses he wore over his too-small eyes were always covered with film. The way his top lip never quite closed completely and his fingers never stopped moving. Those were the things that kept Donald from ever seeming like a teenager.

"Do you want to play handball? I brought a ball." Donald ran a hand nervously through the hair on the back of his head and then chirped slightly.

"No," I said, walking toward my bike. "Let's just go home." Without argument, Donald headed toward his own bike.

I hadn't bothered to lock mine up, so I got on quickly and started riding away before Donald even started fiddling with the combination on his lock. He had trouble memorizing the numbers, so he kept them written down on a card in his wallet. He was fishing for the card when two big boys rode past me on racing bikes. The wind from their passing and the whir of their tires forced me to turn to watch them. At the speed the boys were going, there was no way they could avoid hitting Donald.

"Ten points for the 'tard'!" one screamed out.

"Easy shot!" the other replied. They picked up speed.

That's when I realized they were aiming for Donald on purpose!

2

Bullies

Donald didn't see them coming.

Even though the boys shouted horrible names at him, my brother remained completely oblivious to it all, concerned only with his combination lock.

"Lame brain!"

"Dork head!"

The noise around him made it hard for him to concentrate on the numbers. He turned the card over and over, brought his hands to his ears, pushed his glasses tightly against his nose. I knew this behavior. He was more worried about not getting the combination right than what was going on around him. He was worried to death about it.

But he couldn't afford to be right then.

"Donald! Watch out!" I screamed.

Donald looked up, but it was too late to get away. His bike blocked any exit. All he could do was cringe.

Inches in front of my brother, the boys skidded to a stop, leaving long black marks on the sidewalk. Even though they were probably only fourteen or fifteen years old, up on their bikes the boys towered over crouching Donald. They laughed at their joke. Donald gave them that nervous smile. What could he say? What could he do? Donald didn't know how to fight back. Even if he did, these guys would clobber him.

"Get away from him!" I shouted. I ditched my bike and ran up behind the bullies. They swung around toward me. Like my brother, I felt pretty helpless with these guys. I was only eleven, so they were older and stronger. If I had to fight, I would. I was ready. I had teeth and nails. I might not have won, but I could do some damage. "Leave him alone. He's not doing anything to you."

"Are you his babysitter?" the taller boy asked, his chuckles sounding like he was choking on milk.

"Are you a retard like him?" the one wearing his cap backwards snickered.

Nothing grated on my nerves more than that word. Donald was not a "retard."

"Get away," I seethed.

The boys snickered at me. "Ooh, tough girl." They tugged their scratched-up bikes around so the front wheels aimed right at me. The taller boy faked as though he would run me over. I made the mistake of flinching.

"Better get yourself another bodyguard," he shouted to Donald, never taking his mean eyes off of me.

Donald stood up behind them. "That's my sister," he informed them. "Not my bodyguard."

"Your sister," they both commented.

"Are you a retard too?" one asked. "How do you spell dumb-head?"

"Leave us alone," I said quietly.

"Or what?"

"Or I'll pop your tires." I raised a hand to the stick-pin on my shirt shaped like a soccer ball. I won that pin in a tournament a month ago and always wore it. Quickly, I unfastened it and pointed the sharp end at the front tires of the bikes.

"Ooh, we're scared," they both teased. The taller boy reached out and grabbed the pin from my hand. It had to have stabbed his palm, but he didn't show any sign of it hurting. He threw the pin far into the grass. With an evil grin to me, he nodded to his friend, and they rode away. Over their shoulders they called out, "Next time we won't stop!"

I unlocked Donald's bike lock with shaky fingers while Donald poked around the grass looking for the pin.

"Do you know them?" I asked.

"Matt Tonkovich and Daryl Peck. Daryl Peck is the bigger one. He lives on Sego Street. Near our house."

I held the bike for Donald to get on. He ignored me and kept looking through the grass. I asked him, "Are they always so mean to you?"

11

"Not always." He said that about everyone. "No," he denied.

"When are they nice?" I pushed.

"Sometimes," he answered, but Donald was already thinking about something else. "Do you want to go for a shake today? I'd like a chocolate shake."

"No." It was always no. "Not today. I just want to go home."

I didn't tell my brother that I didn't want to be seen with him any longer that day. It was bad enough that Donald was picked on all the time. I didn't like it happening to me too.

"Get on your bike already," I ordered.

Donald stood up and walked toward the bike as if he wasn't sure that was what he wanted to do.

"What is it?" I asked.

"Don't you want your pin?"

I did want my pin. Earning it had taken a lot of work. Now it was doomed to be a surprise prick in the foot to some barefooted two-year-old.

"We'll never find it," I told him halfheartedly, and I figured that was half true. Donald certainly wouldn't be able to find it, and I didn't have the patience to help him look. Besides, what if Matt and Daryl came back?

I fetched my bike from where I'd left it lying in the middle of the sidewalk and led the way home. Everything Donald saw sparked an observation he had to make out loud, but I didn't say a word in response to him. Donald never clued in that I just wanted him to shut up.

3

The Girls

"**M**y mom said I could have a sleepover for my birthday," Jackie announced to the four of us sharing the shaded end of the lunch table. "I started making invitations last night. Only nine people can come."

Jackie had this tendency to be, well, snotty. I didn't like her very much, but everyone else liked her, so what choice did I have but to pretend that Jackie was okay?

"Nine girls. That's easy." LaQuita figured it out, using her purple-tipped fingers. "Us four, of course. Invite Patty

13

because she'll bring her make-up. Oh, and Tricia, because if she comes the boys will try to spy on us."

"The boys will come either way," Cathy said. "They'll try to scare us like they did at Stacy's party."

Jackie looked over at the boys sitting impatiently with finished lunches, waiting for the whistle that allowed everyone to get up and play in the yard. She sneered. "I don't want any boys coming over at all. They ruin everything."

"Not everything," Stacy said, grinning. LaQuita smacked her lightly on the back of her head.

After taking a long sip from her juice box, Jackie looked up at me and nodded. "What do you think, Heidi, Heidi, Heidi Ho? Who should I invite?"

I put down my sandwich and avoided Jackie's eyes. "Is this a test?" I asked after I swallowed a bite.

Unfortunately, Jackie heard me. "Do you have a problem?"

"No," I said quickly. "I just think you should pick whoever you want. It doesn't matter to me."

"What if I don't invite you?" Jackie threatened.

"Then I won't go," I answered. I tossed the rest of my sandwich in the trashcan. It was a shot none of the other girls could make. One of the boys called over, "Nice one, Hide!"

"Maybe you shouldn't invite Heidi," Stacy suggested. She was such a popularity leech. "She's just like a boy but not in the fun ways."

I adjusted the straps on my overalls. I really didn't care what Stacy thought.

Did I?

Cathy leaned over and whispered into my ear, "You're ruining this for us."

It took some effort, but I prevented myself from rolling my eyes. "I'm not trying to cause a fight," I explained to the other girls. "It just doesn't matter to me who you invite to your party. If you need nine girls, invite your two sisters, the four of us, Patty, and Tricia. There."

"Not a bad list," LaQuita admitted. She was braiding Stacy's straight brown hair so they could look like twins. It was an impossible feat, however, since LaQuita's hair was short, black, and curly.

The whistle blew, and the boys took off like dogs released from their leashes. They headed for the basketball court. I wanted to go too, but when I motioned to get up, Jackie snapped at me, "We're not done, Hide."

Uncomfortably, I settled back into my part of the picnic table bench. I straddled it so both of my canvas tennis shoes touched the floor. The discarded piece of aluminum foil on the table in front of me became a ball for me to play with between my knees on the bench. The other girls were still talking about the party. I wasn't listening.

"Do any of you want to play dodgeball?" I interrupted.

Jackie scowled at me. LaQuita scrunched up her lips and nose. Stacy swiped her bangs out of her eyes so I could more effectively see the displeasure in them. Cathy looked at the table, embarrassed.

"Not today," Jackie said after a moment. "We're not doing that anymore."

So why was I even sitting with them? Dodgeball was the only reason I even got inducted into the popular circle. A year before I couldn't have cared less what Jackie or anyone else thought of me. In fifth grade I'd been best friends with Bobby Cippola, a shrimpy guy but a great runner. Bobby moved over the summer, basically leaving me alone in a world of girls who didn't play sports and boys who didn't like being around girls.

Two weeks after school started, I got to know Cathy Liang. She was a sweet, shy girl who had always been pretty quiet and unnoticed. So it was a surprise when I saw her beating kid after kid on the handball court one morning during recess. She had some definite skill at the game, and she even made *me* sweat as I attempted to get her out. Our match went on so long that everyone waiting for a turn finally gave up and walked away. Only the bell made us quit, and we called it a tie. We'd been friends ever since. Cathy soon began calling me her best friend, but I had trouble going that far.

Cathy had an obsession with Jackie, LaQuita, and Stacy. More than anything in the world, she wanted to hang out with them. Surprisingly, it was me who made it possible.

During September and October, the sixth-grade teachers had all four sixth-grade classes play dodgeball tournaments during P.E. It was really popular among the boys, and at lunch they'd continue whatever game they'd started during class. The girls hated to play because the boys threw the ball so hard that it hurt.

I got frustrated by the whole situation. Girls played like wimps in class just so they'd get out quicker and didn't play at all during lunch. To solve the problem, I asked my teacher whether I could start an all-girl dodgeball tournament. No boys allowed.

Well, nothing grabs the interest of popular girls more than a "no boys allowed" rule. Girls came running. In fact, the girls' tournament was more of a hit than the boys' tournament. It was great for a while. I became instantly popular, and I took Cathy happily along for the ride. It helped that she was really good at dodgeball too.

By December, whoever wasn't playing the game was watching it. Every day a big crowd gathered around to cheer or jeer us on. Little by little the boys started abandoning their own games and came to watch ours. That left the super athletes like Tim, Rick, and Martin out on the fields by themselves.

On the morning everything changed, those three guys were standing to the side of the court, Tim tossing a basketball back and forth in his hands. I could hear him trying to convince his friends to come join him at the basketball court, but no one was listening to him. Our dodgeball game had come down to just Jackie and me facing off. Whoever got hit first would lose. I had the ball in my hands and threw it hard. Jackie ducked out of the way just in time, but her team wasn't fast enough behind her to catch it. The ball snapped right into the hands of Martin. An evil grin spread across his face, and after a nod from Tim, he sailed that ball right at Jackie. It got her square in the back. The smacking sound was painful to hear, and I could only imagine what it felt like. Jackie crumbled to her knees on the asphalt and started screaming and crying.

The lunch monitor, Ms. Tillman, came running to see what the problem was. Practically the whole sixth grade saw what happened, so the boys didn't get away with it. They sure tried, though. While LaQuita and Stacy helped Jackie to the nurse, Martin, Tim, and Rick went into this whole sob story about how the all-girls dodgeball game wasn't fair. Boys should get to play if they wanted to.

Ms. Tillman agreed with the boys. Before sending them to the tables to sit out the rest of recess, she told me, "You have to be fair and let everyone play who wants to."

"But you don't understand . . ." I tried.

"The boys play or no game," Ms. Tillman said. So the games petered out. No one wanted to play if the boys were going to ruin it. Sad thing was, the boys really never had any intention of playing at all. They just wanted to stop the girls' tournament. And they succeeded.

Now I was stuck at the lunch table every lunch hour, every recess, every free time, gossiping and chatting. The girls braided each other's hair. They painted each other's fingernails. They traded shoes. I didn't ever participate. I just watched. Lucky me.

"When is your birthday, Hide?" Stacy asked.

I snapped out of my reverie. "February 16th. Why?"

"Are you going to have a party?"

I looked up through the strand of hair that had crept across my face. All the girls were eagerly looking at me. Had they all been planning each other's parties the whole time? I really had been zoning, hadn't I?

"No, I probably won't," I answered. "I was thinking about going to a hockey game with my dad and brother."

"You know," LaQuita said, leaning across the table, "you only get so many chances a year to throw a party."

"True," Jackie agreed. "And only so many chances a year to force your friends to buy presents for you."

18

I smiled weakly. "I just don't think I want a party this year. I'd rather go to yours."

"I think you should throw a party," Cathy said. "It would give us all a chance to see where you live."

"You don't know where she lives?" Jackie said to Cathy. It was an amazing discovery for her. "You're her best friend. You've never been to her house?"

"She's never invited me," Cathy said quietly. With Jackie it was difficult to know how to respond sometimes. It was hard to tell whether she was ripping on you or just asking you an honest question.

"Has Heidi been to *your* house?" LaQuita pressed, those deep brown eyes of hers focusing more on me than Cathy.

"Yes, I have," I answered for my friend to remind them all that I was still there and able to speak.

"So what's up with that?" Jackie asked.

"I don't have a lot to do at my house," I told them. "Cathy's closer to school, and she has a pool and better video games. It's no big deal."

"No big deal," Jackie said, "but hardly fair."

"Personally, I think it stinks," Stacy said.

"Well, Cathy, I think you should go over to Heidi's house. Find out what she's been hiding from you." Jackie looked at LaQuita and Stacy and burst out laughing. "Get it? Hide's hiding something. Ha ha! Yes! You've earned your nickname at last, Hide."

"I feel so honored," I said under my breath so none of them would hear me. I didn't think I was hiding anything from them on purpose. Not really. I hadn't told any of them things about my home life become no one needed to know about it.

It wasn't their business. After all, I didn't know much about their lives outside of school.

"So, ladies," Jackie said, calming down from her hysterics, "when will the big playdate be?"

Cathy looked at me and shrugged. "I don't care."

I studied my broken fingernails.

"Okay, I'll decide," Jackie announced. "You two shall have a playdate at Hide's house on Friday afternoon, starting at 3:30. I think it should be a sleepover too."

I hated how Jackie kept emphasizing the word "playdate" like we were still in kindergarten.

"It's up to Cathy when she'd like to *hang out* with me," I said. I knew Cathy wouldn't want to sleep over once she met. . .

"Then it's set," Jackie said, hitting the table with the palm of her hand. "Oh, I'm so excited. Be sure to tell us all about it, won't you, Cathy?"

"I'm sure there won't be much to tell," Cathy said.

I turned away from the girls and stared out at the playground. *I'm sure you'll have plenty to tell,* I thought. *More than enough.*

4

Friday Afternoon

"Cathy is my friend, not yours," was the first thing I said to Donald when I walked through the front door of our house Friday afternoon. "That means you need to leave us alone." No "hello" or "how was your day." Just the facts.

"Uh, hi," Cathy said, nodding to Donald as she passed him in the front hallway.

"Brunette," Donald muttered in response. He was looking at Cathy's hair. It was in a long ponytail down her back. I could see Donald's fingers twitching to touch it, so I quickly ushered my friend into the TV room.

I said to my brother as we passed by, "Donald, if you want to be helpful, you can get us some sodas."

"Okay."

There was a ton of clanging about in the kitchen. Enough noise to keep Cathy and me from starting our visit with each other. Once or twice the voice of my mother broke through to say, "Slow down, Donald." A few minutes later, Donald reappeared with two tall glasses of soda and ice cubes, full to the rims.

"Thanks," Cathy said, carefully taking a glass from Donald. He put a coaster on the coffee table for her. A couple of drops of soda landed on a magazine before I grabbed the tilted second glass from him. I put my drink on the magazine rather than on a coaster.

Donald hovered over us, not saying anything. His eyes darted from my face to my glass. Back and forth. It was clear that Donald was bothered by something.

"What do you want, Donald?" I asked impatiently.

"A ring. You'll make a ring on the magazine." He pointed to the magazine.

"So?"

"It ruins the magazine. You should use a coaster." He picked up an extra coaster and held it in front of me with one hand. His other hand twitched and snapped nervously at his side.

I took the coaster and transferred the glass. With a napkin, I wiped up the water ring left on the glossy cover girl's face as best I could. Donald straightened up and breathed better.

"Are you happy now?" I asked him, handing him the wet napkin.

"Huh?" His mind had already leapt to something else.

"Forget it."

Donald gazed out the window to the yard and then back at Cathy. "Do you like butterflies?"

I had to look. I craned my neck to see whether there was a butterfly in the garden. Nope. Not a single one. Of course there wasn't a butterfly out there. It was often a complete mystery where Donald found his topics of incongruous conversation.

"Yeah, I like butterflies," Cathy answered. "Who doesn't?" Her smile was forced as if she were trying to get the punchline of an unfunny joke. I recognized that look. I'd seen it on so many people's faces when dealing with Donald. It meant Donald had better beat it, and soon, before he irritated the spit out of her.

"Do you know how they're born?" Donald asked.

"They come from caterpillars," Cathy said to oblige him. "I learned that in, like, first grade. Maybe preschool."

Oh no, I thought. Cathy thought Donald was treating her like a baby. She didn't get it.

"No," Donald argued, though his tone was anything but nasty. "They come from cocoons. The cocoons come from caterpillars. The caterpillars come from larvae—"

"Donald, is this a test?" I asked him.

"No." Donald switched his gaze to me as though I'd pulled him out of a trance.

"Are you asking questions you know the answers to?"

Donald shuffled his feet. "Yes," he mumbled.

"Stop it."

Donald closed his mouth as much as he could for a person who couldn't close his lips properly. He crouched down beside the table, put one elbow on the wooden surface, and clicked his fingers against my soda glass. He watched the two of us, waiting for us to talk.

Cathy had the look of wanting to start a real conversation, but she kept flicking glances over at Donald. Most people would've gotten the message that they weren't wanted. Donald didn't understand subtlety.

"Is he going to stay in here the whole time?" Cathy finally asked.

"No." I looked hard at my brother. "Can't you tell that we want you to go away?" Donald clicked his fingers and smiled nervously. Sure he could tell, but he didn't know what else to do. He needed alternatives. "Why don't you take a bike ride to the store or play with the dog in the backyard?"

"Can I watch TV?" Donald asked.

I felt myself turning red and tried to breathe calmly so I wouldn't lose my cool. Imagine a sixteen-year-old asking permission from an eleven-year-old. Cathy must've thought he was insane.

"I guess," I sighed. We only had one family TV, and it was in that room. The only other TV was in my parents' bedroom, and we weren't allowed to sit in there. I knew he wanted to watch TV just so he could stay near Cathy and her long hair.

Donald picked up the remote control, and after several attempts he managed to get the thing turned on and set to the channel he wanted. He liked to watch the news. I thought the news was boring, and I didn't know whether Donald really enjoyed it or watched it because it made him appear smarter. A lot of times Donald would do things like that: look at newspapers, clip coupons, thumb through reference books just to make it look like he was doing something intelligent.

With Donald now on the floor in front of the TV, engrossed with the short attention span reports about theft, murder, and arrests, Cathy and I could finally start our visit with each other. We talked about which teachers we hated the most and what it was going to be like when we finally got to start junior high.

"My cousin is in sixth grade and is already in middle school," Cathy told me. "I'm so jealous."

"I don't know," I commented. "I kind of like being in elementary school one extra year. Junior high seems scary. Everyone's so tall."

Cathy opened her mouth to say something, but Donald abruptly jumped to his feet cheering and making all kinds of strange whooping noises. On the TV a sports announcer was showing clips of the latest games. Donald had his hands balled up into fists at his sides, and he stomped his feet on the floor. His broad smile left no doubt about how excited he was.

I liked to see Donald happy. Usually. Today, however, it was annoying.

"Donald, be quiet," I shouted at him.

Donald sat down, but he didn't get any quieter.

"Donald," I repeated, heavier this time. "We're trying to talk."

Donald twisted his body so he could look back at us. He didn't say anything, and the blank look on his face showed that he couldn't remember why he was looking at us. I'd merely distracted him.

Uncomfortably, Cathy tucked her stray hairs behind her ears. "Do you want something?" Donald didn't say anything. "Take a picture. It lasts longer."

I sneered at my friend. I couldn't stop myself. For years I'd protected Donald. No one got away with being rude to him, no matter how bizarre he got.

Before she could say anything, though, Donald spoke up.

"Brunette."

This was the worst. I could tell Donald was on the verge of getting up so that he could touch Cathy's hair. This was a habit the whole family was working really hard at getting him to quit.

"Cathy, maybe we should go upstairs to my room," I suggested.

"Maybe I should just go home," Cathy responded. She stood up and grabbed her backpack. "I have a lot of homework to do anyway."

"It's Friday," I said, but I knew what Cathy was trying to tell me: she wanted to get away from Donald. She would never come back over to play again. I wasn't even sure that Cathy would invite me over to her house again. It wouldn't be a very fair friendship if Cathy had to do all the hosting. "Maybe we can meet at the movies this weekend—or at the park?" I tried to come up with some kind of compromise. A solution.

"I like movies," Donald piped in.

"I wasn't talking to you," I snapped at my brother. He'd done enough damage already. To Cathy I said, "We could go tomorrow. I'll pay for both of us."

"Tomorrow is Saturday," Donald interrupted.

"So?" I said.

"We go to the park on Saturday."

"We'll skip it," I snapped at him. "You'll survive."

"You take your brother to the park?" Cathy scrunched up her face, looking repulsed by the idea.

I didn't answer that. I didn't know what words to use that wouldn't make it worse in her opinion. I watched my brother grin that sad grin of his and turn back to the TV. I felt immediately guilty even though I wasn't sure how much I had really hurt his feelings. It was always hard to tell what went in and what just bounced off.

"I think I'll skip the movies this weekend," Cathy said. "I have stuff to do."

I didn't bother to persist. What was the point? Cathy made it clear that she was done with me for the time being. Maybe Cathy just needed some time to get over the shock of Donald. Maybe, eventually, Cathy would just get over it and decide it didn't matter that my brother was a little different. I hoped for that, anyway.

"All right," I said, sighing, and I showed Cathy to the door. "You want me to ride partway to your house with you?"

"No, I don't think so," Cathy said, getting on her bike, which had been leaning against the side of the house. "I think I'm going to stop by Jackie's for a little bit. She said she had a dress she didn't want anymore, and if I came by she would give it to me."

I nodded that I understood. Jackie. Cathy would tell Jackie all about Donald. Once the most popular girl at school had that nugget of gossip, what would that do to my reputation?

I tried to put the concern out of my mind as I watched Cathy pedal down the street, but I couldn't do it. It was pretty clear that my friendship with Cathy was doomed.

5

The Notes

Dear Heidi,

You're selfish and stuck up, and nobody wants to be friends with you anymore.

The note wasn't signed. I couldn't even tell who'd passed it to me. I'd been reading, and when I looked up from my book, the note was on my desk. Free reading time on Mondays meant the kids in class could move about in order to fetch books from the bookshelves or borrow passes to go to the library. The substitute teacher, Ms. Hill, wasn't very good at keeping everyone from talking, which bothered me because I kept getting distracted from reading an awesome book about the discovery of the bones of an unknown species and the suspicion that they came from aliens who had visited Earth thousands of years ago. The movement and the noise of my classmates drove me crazy.

And then the note.

Stuck up? I had never acted stuck up. At least I didn't think I'd ever acted stuck up. Maybe I bragged about sports, but I really was the best girl athlete in the sixth grade. People complimented me about my ability a lot, but I tried not to go on and on about it, no matter how proud I felt. Usually I just said thank you, and that had always seemed right.

Was that what the note meant? If so, why now? I hadn't done anything braggy or worth accepting a compliment over lately. Why didn't someone give me this note months ago when I was organizing the dodgeball games? I was kind of showing off then. I didn't even wear my soccer pin anymore.

Also, the note said I was being selfish. About what? What did I have that I wasn't sharing? I was so confused, and I wished that whoever wrote the note had just put his or her name on it so I could ask what I'd done wrong and fix it. If I could prevent someone from being mad at me, I'd like to try. Clearly, whoever wrote the note intended to stay mad and didn't want the problem resolved at all.

I considered showing the note to Ms. Hill privately, but then I figured that, as a substitute, she wouldn't have the slightest clue what to do about it. To wait until the next day when Ms. Overstreet came back might be too late to change anything. Besides, if the person who sent the note found out I'd shown it to a teacher, he or she might get even madder.

Showing it to Jackie was an option. If anyone would know who'd written it, she would. Jackie knew all the gossip, who hated who, and all of that kind of stuff. But what if it was Jackie who'd sent it?

Now that I thought of it, that made the most sense. Sure. I had no doubt that on Friday afternoon Cathy had run off to tell Jackie all about how weird Donald was, and now Jackie was tormenting me.

But why stuck up? Why selfish? It would have made more sense if Jackie had written something mean about Donald.

Another note dropped on my desk.

I looked up immediately to see who left it. I still couldn't tell, but I caught a flash of LaQuita plopping into her seat and Stacy peeking over the top of her book to see whether I'd read it.

It's a conspiracy, I thought. *They're all out to get me.*

I opened the note.

Dear Heidi,

We heard about your deep, dark secret. You should have shared.

Again, it was unsigned. I didn't need a signature this time to know for sure who'd written it. I looked up at Jackie, who kept her eyes on her book while twirling her long brown hair around her fingers. Jackie wasn't really reading. She was just playing innocent. I knew her well enough to tell. Stacy and LaQuita snickered from their side-by-side desks, and I wished Ms. Hill would move them apart. I searched the room for Cathy, who was mysteriously absent. At the library maybe? Did she know what Jackie was doing?

I slouched in my seat and propped up my book on my desk so it would block my view of them or the possibility of any of them seeing my face. With effort, I squinted to focus on the sentences on the page and what they could possibly mean if I were really reading them. It was all gobbledy-gook because my ears were busy listening for whispers of my name, and sensors on my body were on high alert for anyone who might be passing close to my desk. A wisp of air and a soft click on my desk, tiny sounds that shouldn't have been heard over the noise of the chatter in the room, were like bomb blasts to me. I lowered my book to find another note on my desk, this one disguised as a paper airplane. Someone had tossed it, and I had no idea who.

I unfolded the note. This one had different handwriting. Messier. No bubbly letters with circles instead of periods. It was almost hard to read, but the signature wasn't. I read that first.

Kirk.

Kirk? This had to be a joke.
I read the words he'd supposedly scribbled.

Hide,
Do you want to hang out sometime? Maybe a movie with me on Saturday?

A *date*? I was being asked out on a date by the best basketball player in the school? By the boy with the curly black hair? By the boy who actually *combed* his curly black hair?

Nah. That couldn't be it. His note said "hang out," so I took that to mean it was just an invitation to become better friends. No one went on dates in sixth grade. Mostly when boys and girls decided to be a *thing*, all they did was pass notes and talk on the phone at night. Jackie said sometimes her parents dropped her off to meet a boy for lunch or to stroll around the park for a while.

So I twisted around in my seat, intending to smile and nod at Kirk instead of bothering to write him a note in return. However, his face was bright red, and he struggled to keep his eyes hidden behind his paperback horror novel. Tim, his best friend, sat behind him and kept poking him in the back with the eraser of his pencil. Finally irritated enough, Kirk reached back and swiped the pencil out of Tim's hand. Tim merely laughed harder. Kirk hazarded a look around his book at me and then went back to reading.

Okay, he was acting a little sheepish. If all he wanted was to be my friend, I didn't think he'd be weird like that. Only a couple of girls in the sixth grade had boyfriends already. Jackie, obviously. Every boy in the school had a crush on the girl who wore make-up and had begun to grow a figure, and she'd already broken the hearts of two of them. Stacy went steady with Aaron Giles for two weeks. There were a couple of girls in Ms. Stemple's class who were always holding hands with boys on the playground during recess. Of course, all the girls had crushes on someone or other, but most of the boys weren't super into girls yet.

I thought about how I must look right then. It was still early in the day, and I was sleepy. My hair was hanging in front of my eyes like it often did because I didn't have bangs and hated headbands. My fingernail polish had mostly flaked off. I didn't like to wear skirts, so I wore my denim capris. Though I wore my favorite t-shirt, it was covered by my dad's dingy gray college sweatshirt, which I kept on because the classroom was always freezing cold.

Boys didn't ask girls like me out on dates. They asked well-dressed, pretty girls like Stacy and LaQuita. Or popular girls like Jackie. I went back to my original thought: Kirk wasn't asking me on a *date* date. Just a buddy thing. Yeah. That made more sense. He was just all red and embarrassed because Tim was making a big deal out of it.

Stacy and LaQuita's chatting got louder. It was easy to hear that they were talking about the third note I'd received. They wanted to know what it said. I looked at them and then down at the invitation again. Why didn't Kirk ask one of them to the movies? If I were a boy, I would have. They were so much prettier and more popular than me.

That was it.

He didn't really ask me out, buddy or no. He wouldn't. I bet that Jackie put him up to this tease because she knew how much I liked Kirk. A cruel joke.

I scribbled a note of my own then, certain that if I passed a note it would be the one to be discovered by Ms. Hill. I took the chance anyway and lucked out.

Dear Kirk,
    I don't think it's very funny.
                                    Heidi

34

6

My Turn to Be Mean

"**H**ide! Wait!"

No. I didn't want to talk to him. I didn't want to talk to anybody. I'd purposely avoided Kirk, Jackie, and the others all day long. More notes had been passed to me, but I refused to even open them let alone answer them. Instead I made a big show of dropping each one into the trashcan.

It had been such a long day. I'd found it nearly impossible to stay in the classroom with so many eyes focusing on me. All kinds of excuses to leave the room filled my head, and I acted on most of them. First, I went to the library to look at encyclopedias for my history report. The bathroom got frequent unnecessary visits. I told Ms. Hill that I had diarrhea. The water fountain was a good excuse even though I never drank from it. I offered to clean the art room. I volunteered to take the attendance to the office. I even stuck my hand up to help in the cafeteria at lunch so I wouldn't have to sit at the lunch table. Ms. Hill must have grown tired of handing me the hall pass.

There were times when the note passers couldn't be avoided. The line. Free time in the classroom. P.E. But I stayed as quiet as possible, and since Jackie and the others were having so much fun with their "anonymous" notes, they didn't speak about it either. Kirk avoided my eyes all day. Maybe he felt bad. I hoped he did.

So that's why I rushed home after school. I actually ran out of the classroom seconds before the dismissal bell rang, with Ms. Hill hollering after me to stop. I didn't want to face anyone. If I could have ridden my bike home with my eyes shut, I would have.

And I didn't care that Kirk was calling my name. Pretending like I didn't hear him, I left him far behind, wondering what the expression on his face looked like.

I was a fast bike rider when I wanted to be, so I sped all the way home, taking shortcuts and rushing dangerously through stop signs. Luckily traffic wasn't typically a problem at 3:00, and drivers tended to be extra careful because they expected kids to do exactly the crazy kind of riding I was doing.

I was within blocks of my house when I heard a noise that made me want to scream.

"Whoo-hoo! Ooo-yip! Ooo-yip!"

Donald.

He was close by, riding home from school too. As usual, he was sounding off. He enjoyed riding his bike. That's what the strange sounds meant. Maybe he saw a dog and was imitating its bark. Maybe he was making sounds for the gnats flying in his face. Maybe he was singing along with his squeaky bicycle chain or the wind rushing past his ears. Who could know? All I knew was that I didn't want Donald to see me. Couldn't I have just a few moments of peace?

No.

"Heidi!" Donald called. He rushed up to meet me. His white helmet was practically falling off of his head, and his pant legs were stuffed inside his tube socks to keep them from getting stuck in the chain. I didn't acknowledge him. Donald didn't seem to notice.

"Did you just get out of school?" he asked.

"No," I said sarcastically, the way I always did when Donald asked questions that he didn't need to ask. "I just got off a train. I've been traveling with the circus all weekend. Didn't you notice I was gone?"

Donald stared at me for a second, processing my words. If he ever got my sense of humor, he didn't show it. All he did was focus back on the road in front of him. "I just got out of school too."

"I know," I said. "Where else would you be coming from?"

Some teenagers drove by in a yellow car and catcalled out the window at us. Their words were a blur, just like their faces, but I knew the words hadn't been kind. Something about the baby on his bike.

37

Donald squinted into the sun. "Daryl Peck."

One of the bullies from the park. Neither of those guys who bothered us was old enough to drive, but they certainly could have friends with licenses. Too bad Donald couldn't drive. He could run over their stupid bikes when they were stuck without their car-driving friends. The image of Daryl Pike and Matt Tonkovich spread out on the asphalt like cartoon characters made me burp up a giggle.

I wondered whether Donald ever had gonna-get-you-back notions. With the amount he'd been picked on, it would seem likely. Probably not Donald, though. He was too gentle.

I, on the other hand, desperately wanted to get back at Cathy and the kids at school. It was all I could think of as I pedaled along. I didn't know how yet, so I took my anger out on Donald. It was all his fault anyway.

"Race you home," I suggested. He took me up on it, and I was glad. There was no way his gawky legs could ever pedal that ten-speed of his as fast as I could go on my cruiser. He was dust in my tracks in no time.

When I got home, I jumped off my bike while it was still moving and shoved it carelessly against the inside wall of the garage. I ran inside and locked the door leading from the garage to the house. A moment later I heard Donald's whooping noises nearing the house. He'd lost the race, but he didn't care.

I sat down on the family room couch and flipped on the TV. Mom wasn't home from work yet, so no one would care if I caught a couple of my favorite cartoons.

Donald's bike squeaked loudly as he squeezed the brakes. I could hear him clinking around in the garage, trying to maneuver his bicycle against the wall next to mine. I could picture him trying to figure out the best way to place his bike so there would be room for Mom's car when she got home from work. Anyone would know that my bike just needed to be pushed forward a little, but Donald wouldn't be able to reach that conclusion. He would knock things over and push and prod at his own bike until, at last, he would give up, and Mom would complain about it later.

No, I wouldn't go out and help him. No, I didn't feel sorry for him. I'd done this on purpose. It was high time Donald started to think like a sixteen-year-old—or at least like an eleven-year-old. Maybe by getting in trouble enough he might learn something. I was so tired of him being my "baby" brother.

The ruckus stopped outside. After fifteen minutes, Donald had finally given up. Now a new challenge awaited him. He didn't know how to unlock the door. Sure, he knew how to turn a key in a knob, but this door was more difficult than most. To unlock it, the knob had to be pulled as it was turned. It was harder than a baby-proof medicine jar. Donald could never get the hang of it, no matter how many times he practiced with Dad, Mom, or me.

He tried the knob. When it didn't turn, he knocked on the door. I didn't budge. I pretended like I couldn't hear it.

"Heidi," Donald called. "Heidi, I'm home. Can you unlock the door?"

I stared straight ahead at the TV, but I didn't know what the villain on the screen was talking about. All I heard was Donald.

"Heidi?"

He made a funny sound like "Zzhhwuu." That meant he was preparing to do something that was tough for him. There was a bumping against the door and then the sound of a zipper. Donald was getting his key out of his backpack. A jingling preceded the sound of Donald fitting the key in the lock. So far so good.

Then the twist. And the stop. Twist. Stop. Jiggle. Jiggle. Twist. Take the key out and put it back in again. Twist. Stop. Jiggle. Jiggle.

"Heidi?" He knocked on the door again. "Heidi can you open the door? Heidi?"

I could hear the panic in his voice. I wondered whether he had to go to the bathroom. He could, of course, go to the front door, which was easier to open. *Or* he could go to the sliding glass door in the back, but he wouldn't think to do either of those things. He was pretty much stuck.

I let him fuss for another few minutes before guilt wore me down. Mom would be home soon, and she would get really mad at me for locking my brother out of the house. She wouldn't understand.

I got up and dragged myself to the garage door. I opened it to find Donald's hand still attached to the knob on the outside. He swung into the house with the door, losing his balance and falling to one knee.

"I couldn't do the lock," he said.

"Oh, sorry. I was in the bathroom. I didn't realize I'd locked you out."

Any normal brother would have seen right through me. Any normal brother might have threatened to kill me. But not Donald. He smiled and stood up.

"That's okay."

He didn't mention the bikes. He may have forgotten about them already.

I left him and went back to the couch. Donald went past me to take his backpack to his room. Moments later I heard him in the kitchen making himself a snack. A peanut butter sandwich. Always. Every afternoon. The same thing. I called out, "Can you bring me a soda?"

"Sure," Donald called back. "In a can or glass?"

"Can is fine," I said. One thing that was good about Donald: he made an awfully good servant.

Just then the phone rang. I was too slow picking it up. Donald got it in the kitchen. Ooh! I hated it when Donald answered the phone. As if he ever got phone calls.

"Uh, hello?" I heard him say in his unsure way. "Heidi? Uh, yeah. She's here . . . Uh, who is this?"

Just give me the phone already, I thought.

"Kirk Mannings?" Donald sounded it out as if the name were a foreign word.

Kirk!

What now?

I grabbed the receiver from the coffee table.

"Get off the phone, Donald," I ordered, covering the mouthpiece with one hand. I heard his voice over the phone and from around the kitchen wall. "It's Kirk Mannings."

"I know, Donald," I said with too much emphasis.

"Isn't his brother Randy Mannings, on the Varsity basketball team? Number 24?"

"What if he is?"

Donald paused, said nothing for a moment, and then finally hung up. I felt like groaning, but I held it in.

"Heidi?" Now Kirk sounded unsure. "Are you there?"

"Yeah. I'm here."

"Look, I wanted to say I was sorry about today. I didn't mean for you to think I was joking."

"You didn't?" I wasn't ready to believe him. How did I know Jackie wasn't standing next to him right then, telling him what to say?

"I meant it about the movies," he said. "I'd really like to go. I'll pay. I'll get popcorn and everything."

Like a date? This was too much. "You don't have to do this. Tell Jackie it isn't funny."

"Jackie?" Kirk sounded honestly confused. "This has nothing to do with Jackie. I just think you're nice is all." He paused. I think he said more than he intended. "So, do you want to go?"

"Saturday?" I confirmed.

"Yeah. We'll pick which movie on Friday at school when the new listings come out, okay?"

"Sounds great," I said. And it really did.

Until Donald walked into the room right after I hung up and informed me, "But we go to the park on Saturday."

"Not this Saturday," I said, grinning, not really interested in Donald's opinion about it. "I'm going to the movies."

"Which movie?" Donald wanted to know.

I knew what he was really asking. He was asking whether he could go with us. I gave my brother a hard look and told him, "None of your business."

But I felt certain that Donald would make it his business.

7

At the Movies

Kirk and I decided to ride our bikes and meet at the movie theater in the shopping center so that we wouldn't have to get our parents involved. This way neither of our parents knew it was a "date," and no one would be given a hard time about it. My parents were used to me going out to play with boys, and Kirk's parents thought he was out with Tom.

We met half an hour before the movie, giving us plenty of time to buy popcorn and change our minds about which movie we wanted to see. We each planned to buy our own boxes so we wouldn't have to touch buttery fingers. It would just be too distracting. It was only a first date, after all.

Having just walked through the lobby door and handed the tickets to the man, I heard a terrible sound.

"Brru-whip!"

Donald.

Surprise! He hadn't told me he was going to the movies when I left home, but I knew somehow or other he would wind up there.

I couldn't see him yet, but there was no doubt about his existence. No one I knew on the planet would make such bizarre sounds in public. I scanned the lobby as closely as I could, looking for my brother. It was ultra-important that I saw him before he saw me.

Nowhere.

Then there, by the refreshments counter. He hadn't taken off his bike helmet yet, and his fanny pack sagged, unzipped, around his tummy. If I knew him, and I did, he was ordering a medium popcorn with extra butter, a hot dog with mustard and ketchup, a large soda that he wouldn't drink, and a small box of chocolate candy, the mint kind. It would cost him a fortune as it always did, and he'd get more of it on him than in him. I could see the refreshments counter person frowning as Donald struggled through the order.

How many times had he done this? It always seemed like the first time—the first time he was making the choices as he squinted at the menu on the wall to read it, the first time he was hearing how much it would cost him and grunting slightly as if the number surprised and disappointed him, the first time he had to take money out of his fanny pack and count it as he deliberated about giving exact change and then wound up just giving the guy a twenty.

"Let's get food," Kirk said, rubbing his hands like a mad scientist. He pinched his lips together so they disappeared into a thin line and made his eyes really big. I laughed at him, but then I cut the laughter off quickly in case my brother heard me. He might recognize the sound of my voice. I began to follow Kirk to the refreshments counter but stopped midway on that too. Popcorn smelled so good, but . . .

"How about you get it," I suggested. I handed him ten dollars.

He handed it back. "I'm buying."

"With what?" I joked. "I bet my allowance is bigger than yours." I handed him the money again, and he accepted it gratefully. "Just get me the same thing you're getting. I should go to the bathroom before the movie. Meet me in there."

Kirk scrunched up his forehead playfully and teased, "In the bathroom?"

I giggled quietly. He was so cute. "No, silly." I waved my ticket stub.

"Oh!" he said, smacking his head. "Forgive me. I was being a retard."

This time I didn't laugh at all at what Kirk said. I burned to correct his choice of words, but I didn't want to ruin our good time. Instead, I bit my lip, pointed at the food counter, and then pointed back toward the restrooms with my thumb. "See ya in a minute."

If Kirk noticed any change in my demeanor, he didn't show it. He marched away, and I lingered to watch him and spy on the efforts of my brother.

Donald had walked away from the counter with a tray full of stuff. The person behind the counter was calling him back to give him his change. It was difficult to watch Donald balance his tray while he turned around and headed back to the counter. How would he put the tray down without spilling anything? How would he pick it up again? Would he remember to put the money in his pack and zip it before he tried to pick up the tray again?

Part of me wanted to go help him. Normally I would have. Today I couldn't. People who used words like "retard" as jokes thought people like Donald were mental cases. Kirk was one of those people. Before, I didn't want Donald to see me because I didn't want his weirdness ruining my good time. Now I knew that if Kirk found out I was related to Donald, it would ruin my chances of being his girlfriend.

While both Donald and Kirk were busy at the counter and not concerned with each other, I slipped off to find some seats. I really had no particular need to go to the bathroom.

Not long after I sat down, Donald entered with Kirk right behind him. I slouched in my seat so Donald couldn't see me while counting on Kirk to seek me out. Donald sat behind me somewhere; I didn't know where exactly because I didn't turn around to look. I only knew that he didn't pass me in the aisle. Kirk found me and sat down on the seat to my left, leaving a spare seat between the aisle and me.

"Did you see that guy at the counter?" Kirk whispered as he doled out the popcorn boxes and drinks.

"What guy?" I asked, feigning that I didn't have the slightest idea who Kirk was speaking about.

"This guy. He was a total mess. He ordered everything on the menu practically, and then he could barely carry it.

Check him out. He's two rows back all covered with mustard and soda. He needs a serious brain check." Kirk was half turned around in the seat pointing out Donald. He kept tapping on my shoulder. "C'mon," he said. "You gotta see him."

"I don't really need to," I said, taking a big handful of popcorn. "You described him well enough."

Kirk slid back into his seat. "Whatever. You're missing out. He's a classic." He looked over my shoulder once more and laughed.

Please don't call him names, I thought. *Please leave him alone.*

"What a dork," Kirk said, actually snorting as he laughed.

I couldn't help it; I turned my head to sneak a peek at my brother. To me, Donald looked just fine. Yeah, he had a drop or two of stuff on him, and he was eating his hot dog from the middle rather than from the end, but he had plenty of napkins. He'd be okay. If Kirk would leave him alone, that is.

"Dude," Kirk called out to him. "Where'd you learn how to eat?"

"Leave him alone, Kirk," I said, a little too loud, a little too sharp.

My face went instantly red.

It was too late. The damage had been done. Donald looked over at Kirk and then down at his hot dog. He put it down on the tray and gulped his bite down without chewing—something he wasn't supposed to do and had worked on repeatedly during his therapy sessions. I was ready to leap over chairs and stop him from choking, but he took a big gulp of his drink and seemed to be fine. That half-smile-half-pain look crept across his face, and he sat there not knowing what to do next. He couldn't keep eating or he'd be picked on, yet he had a whole plate of food.

"Tell him you didn't mean it," I whispered to Kirk urgently. "Tell him."

Kirk seemed pretty confused. "What are you talking about?"

He wasn't going to help.

"Donald," I called over to him. By now the theater was pretty full, so a lot of people were paying attention. "He didn't mean it. Just eat your snack, okay?"

"Do you know him?" Kirk asked, amazed.

"Yeah," was all I said about that.

Donald looked carefully at me. "Heidi?" he asked.

"Are you kidding me?" Kirk said. "This is the best. How does he know your name?"

I kept my eyes on the advertisements on the screen so I wouldn't have to see either of their faces. I said, "Maybe he's like that guy from that movie *Rain Man*—seems really dumb but certain things stick to his head like names and dates. I bet he knows your name too."

"Hey, Donald," Kirk called over to him. "What's my name?"

"Kirk Mannings."

"Wow. Weird." Kirk was pretty awed by that demonstration.

"Can I sit with you, Heidi?" Donald asked.

I sighed. That was exactly what I'd feared. "No, Donald. I think it's better if you stay where you are. That way you don't have to move all your stuff again."

48

But he was already getting up.

"No, Donald," I nearly shouted. "Stay!"

And, of course, just to make everything extra perfect, Daryl Peck and Matt Tonkovich walked in right at that moment. They caught on to what was happening right away.

"Here, doggy! Here, doggy!" Daryl teased half-standing Donald.

Matt reached over and grabbed the box of candy Donald had bought and threw it down the aisle. "Fetch, doggy!"

Donald put down his tray and started toward the aisle so he could, in fact, go fetch his candy. Immediately, I jumped to my feet and got it for him. I moved up the aisle to hand it to my brother, who was being blocked by the bullies.

"Oh, look," Daryl said. "Here's his owner."

"Yeah." Matt laughed and said to me, "Why don't you take him for a walk?"

I didn't care that they were boys and a couple years older than me. I shouted at them, "Why don't *you* take a walk?"

"Ooo-oooh," they both said, pretending to be scared.

The lights dimmed in the theater, and the concessions commercial began to play on the screen.

"You're in my way, pee-brain," Daryl said, pushing me. I wouldn't budge for him.

"Go see another movie," I said.

"*You* see another movie," Daryl snapped back, "and take your mutt with you."

People in the movie theater began yelling at us to be quiet. Kirk jumped to his feet to yank me back to our seats.

"Let the guy protect himself, Heidi," he whispered to me. "You're only gonna get us in trouble."

"You don't understand," I hissed back. To the bullies I shouted one more time, "I mean it! Get out of here!"

As if in response, the two boys were suddenly jerked backwards by two large hands. The theater manager had both of them by the arms and was pulling them toward the lobby. The manager looked at me as he did this. "You'd better come too."

I glanced over at Donald. "Sit down, Donald. Watch the movie. It'll be okay."

Donald hesitated, but when the person behind him also grumbled that he should sit down, Donald finally responded by sitting. Kirk reluctantly followed me and the bullies out the door.

"You don't have to come with me," I whispered to him. "This really isn't your business."

"It didn't have to be yours," Kirk snapped back.

"Well," I stammered, not sure what I should tell him at this point, "it's my business now." I stopped as I opened the door to the lobby. "Just go back and watch the movie. I'll come back in if I can. And if I can't, then I'll wait outside for you."

Kirk frowned. "You're not much of a date, are you?"

"I'll make it up to you."

"Yeah, right."

So Kirk went back to his seat, and I sucked in a big breath of air before going out to meet my brother's enemies head on.

8

Nowhere to Go

"She wouldn't move out of the way so we could sit down," Daryl whined to the manager in the lobby as I stepped up to them.

"They were teasing my brother," I said back, trying not to get that same I-didn't-do-it tone in my voice. "I wanted them to stop."

The manager looked at the boys suspiciously. "This little girl was preventing you from going down the aisle?"

I let the little girl part of his question pass for the moment.

"We didn't want to knock her over," Daryl said. Matt just nodded. "I mean, we could have, but we didn't, 'cause, you know, we didn't want to get in trouble. Everything would have been fine if she'd just moved out of the way."

"Everything would have been fine if you hadn't started teasing my brother and stealing his things from him," I retorted.

The manager switched his doubtful gaze to me now. "Is your brother still in there?" It was kind of hard to hear his voice over the arcade games and the movie themes blaring out from doors that kept opening and closing behind us.

"Yes," all of us answered.

"Who's babysitting him?" the manager asked. He leaned over and put his hands on his knees so he could be face level with me.

"Nobody," I said with a sneer. "He doesn't need a babysitter."

"Yes he does," Matt said with his hand over his mouth as he chuckled at himself.

"I'm afraid I don't understand," the manager said. "You were protecting your brother from these two, but you weren't babysitting him?"

Now it was me who didn't quite understand what was being said. It sounded like he was suggesting that if Donald were old enough to fight his own battles then it should be him out here and not me. Is that what he preferred? Boys fighting each other? If that had happened, would any of them be missing the movie right now?

"My brother has some *problems* with certain skills. You must know him. He's here practically every week." The manager shook his head. Maybe he never stepped outside his office unless there was a problem. "Anyway," I went on, frustrated, "Donald is sixteen, and these guys are always picking on him."

The manager straightened up to his full height. "Well, little girl, from now on, I think you should let your brother take care of himself." He turned to Daryl and Matt. "And I suggest you two choose another place to have your battles."

I couldn't believe what I was hearing. "Are you telling them it's okay for them to beat on my brother—or me?"

"It's not my job to tell them what they can or can't do," the manager said to me. "Only that they can't do it here. I just watch out for my business. If you have a problem with these boys, have your parents call each other or go to the police. It's not my concern. For now, I want you all out of my movie theater."

Daryl and Matt cursed under their breath and whined out loud, but the manager's words were final. He didn't even offer a refund as he ushered us to the door.

"Can I at least go in and tell my friend and my brother what's going on?" I asked.

"No," he said. "I can't have you disrupting the show again. They'll just have to look for you afterward."

I craned my neck to look up at the manager and crossed my arms. "I don't like this," I told him. "I don't plan to ever come to the movies here again, and I'll tell my friends to stay away too."

"Whatever, kid," the manager hummed as he scooted me out the door. He knew my threat was pointless. His business would do just fine without me purchasing a ticket.

The bright light of the sun made me wince as I stepped into it. Even as my eyes adjusted to it, I couldn't rid myself of the pained expression on my face. Over by the bike racks Daryl and Matt were talking to each other, but their eyes stayed steady on me.

I dashed across the parking lot to the fast food place. It would be at least an hour and a half before the movie got out, and I needed something to do until then. Since Kirk was sitting with two heaping boxes of popcorn and I had nothing, a hamburger and fries sounded like a pretty good plan. Unfortunately, Daryl and Matt thought it was a good plan too. They followed me.

Instead of going inside, I paused by the newspaper stand and watched them pass by. They didn't look at me, but it was clear they had followed me on purpose.

Okay. Fast food was out. I crossed the parking lot again. There were still a few options in the shopping center. Ice cream sounded good, so I aimed for the parlor.

On cue, the boys exited the fast food restaurant. I could hear them behind me saying things like, "The food in there sucks" and "Yeah, what a grease-pit." Like they probably ever minded the food there before.

I stepped into the ice cream parlor. So did they. I left. So did they. I went to the doughnut place. So did they. I went to the grocery store. So did they. I even went into the bookstore to browse, only to find them browsing in the magazine section a little bit later.

Feeling panicky and desperate, I did my best to ditch them, creeping toward the front door of the store while they were sneaking peeks at an adult magazine. Just before I left, I caught the bookseller's attention and pointed at the boys over by the magazines so he could see what they were up to. The commotion of them getting caught allowed me to escape unnoticed. I rushed back to the grocery store and ducked into the bathroom. I pulled out my cell phone and called home.

"Mom? Can you come over to the movie theater? It's important. There are these guys here that I think are gonna try to hurt Donald when he comes out of the movies. I need you to take Donald home. . . . Me? I'll be okay. I'll ride home with my friend. They're following me around right now, but they'll stop as soon as you get here."

Mom agreed to drive over in the station wagon as soon as she could. Until then, all I could do was keep dodging the boys. It was exhausting, but I was too scared of them to do anything else. The movie theater manager had all but rooted for them to do exactly what they were doing. Who else in the shopping center would say anything different?

My mom showed up ten minutes later, and I sat with her in the car until people started streaming out of the theater.

Donald and Kirk came out side by side, both looking for the same person, neither acknowledging the other.

I opened the car door and rushed toward them. Daryl and Matt rushed over from the bike racks as well. As requested, my mom drove right up to the front of the theater, so Donald couldn't miss seeing the car. She and I had already put his bike in the back.

"Donald, over here!" I called. The bullies advanced quickly. "Hurry! Mom needs you to go somewhere with her!"

"Where?" Donald didn't hurry well. He just stood, stalled by the confusion. "My bike—"

"Mom has it already! Just go!"

I lunged at him and grabbed his skinny arm, tugging him toward the car. Daryl and Matt were right on Donald's heels. Daryl reached out and grabbed Donald's shirt.

"Let go!" I screamed at him. "He didn't do anything to you!"

My mom honked the horn. Donald saw the open passenger door. "Come on, Donald," she shouted with some fake irritation, like Donald's slowness was really putting her out. "I'm waiting. We have to go."

That was all that was needed. The bullies recognized "parent" and backed off. I was proud of my mom for not making it sound like she had come to the rescue. That would have only made things worse in the long run.

Free from the bullies, I directed Donald to the car as Daryl and Matt slunk back into the crowd, probably hoping my mom wouldn't have had time to recognize their faces.

I leaned over and spoke to my mom through the window. "Thank you."

Mom's frown was pretty severe. "You should come too."

"I'll be all right."

"I'm not so sure . . ."

Then Donald interrupted. "Where are we going?"

I nearly laughed. After all that, Donald still didn't have a clue what was going on. "See ya at home." I waved to my mom and brother. "I won't be too much longer."

Donald rolled up the window before our mother could finish saying goodbye, and a moment later the car rolled away.

I turned around and sighed. Daryl and Matt were gone, as I'd hoped. Kirk, on the other hand, was standing right in front of me with the most terrible sneer on his face.

"That was your brother?"

I felt as though I'd been shot with a stun gun. Words didn't come to my mouth. No explanation filled my head. And after what I'd just been through, I didn't feel the need to defend myself to this kid who called other people "retards."

"Yes," I said at last. I headed toward the bike racks, and Kirk followed.

"So is he brain damaged or what? Did your mom drink when she was pregnant? Did he fall on his head as a baby? Do your folks do drugs?"

I unlocked my bike and said nothing.

"Does it run in the family?"

At that, I raised my eyes to meet his. Kirk really wanted to know. I could tell from the tight features in his face that he was half disgusted and half fascinated by me.

"Donald is Donald," I told him, "and I'm me." I got on my bike. "Are you riding home with me, or is our date finished?" I put finger-quotes up when I said "date."

Kirk dug his hands in his pockets and averted his eyes.

"Never mind," I said, sighing.

I rode off on my bike, leaving Kirk behind still trying to find the right words to dump me without sounding totally rude. I doubted that he would ever come up with the words, "I'm sorry."

57

9

A Teenage Makeover

"**G**o upstairs and talk to him," my mom ordered the moment I got home. "He doesn't understand what happened today. His feelings are hurt because you wouldn't sit with him at the movies."

"Oh, *his* feelings are hurt."

The last thing on Earth I wanted to do was go up to Donald's room and cheer him up. If anything he should be cheering *me* up. After all, who was the one who lost a potential boyfriend after being terrorized by high school boys for two hours? Not Donald. Donald had been allowed to gobble up popcorn and soda while watching a great movie.

There was nothing I could say about the unfairness of it all. Going against Mom's wishes when it came to Donald's welfare was like battling a steamroller.

From the hallway I could hear my brother playing. I could even tell which game he'd chosen for himself. He was playing with his model planes, the click-together kind. The glue kind proved to be too difficult to assemble, and after ruining the tops of his dresser and desk and his comforter, our mom said, "No more." Donald flew the planes about the room, one in each hand. They bombed each other and his bed. I opened the door just in time to see the Stealth Bomber demolish the B-21.

"Whaa-aaa! Shh-krrr-shh!"

Donald didn't stop playing even as I sat down on his bed. He picked up another plane and continued the air battle.

"Nn-yerrrr-rrr-ta-ta-ta-ta!"

"Donald."

"EE-rrrr-lll-shhhhh!"

"Donald."

"Crrr-shhh-pt-pt-pt-pt!"

"Donald!"

Donald looked up and handed me a propeller plane. Then he waved the Stealth at me and announced, "He's winning."

"No, he's not."

"Yes. Yes. See?" Donald showed me the crashed planes all over his room as proof.

"No, that's not what I mean, Donald," I said. "I mean that none of these planes can win a fight because they're toys."

"I know," Donald said. "I'm just playing." He swooped the Stealth down to fire on my plane. "Ee-yrrrr!"

"Stop it."

Donald stopped and stared at me.

"Don't you see what you're doing?"

"Playing?"

"No," I said. "You're being weird. Nobody your age plays with planes like this."

Donald immediately got that look on his face that he got whenever he struggled over his homework in front of our dad. It was immensely painful, and I felt my stomach churn, knowing that I'd been the one to put that painful expression in place.

"They don't?" Donald asked.

I patted the bed so that Donald would sit next to me. Once he was seated, I took the Stealth out of his hand and put it on the floor.

"Do you know why Daryl and Matt pick on you all the time?"

"They're not very nice," Donald said simply.

"Well, yeah," I agreed. "But it's more than that. They pick on you because you act so bizarre all the time."

"I don't mean to."

"I know. That's why I'm going to help you act normal. Just because you learn slowly doesn't mean you have to be a freak."

I looked around Donald's room. The walls were covered with baseball pennants and posters of sports stars. On his shelves were collections of model planes and seashells. In a cup on his desk were fifty mini-flags, one for each state, and a plastic coin counter.

"Let's start with your room."

"Okay."

Donald didn't jump to his feet or anything. I knew that he didn't understand what I was about to do. Typical. Donald would just follow my lead. Hopefully, though, something good would come out of it this time.

"Right now your room looks like it belongs to someone my age or younger. Since you're sixteen and not ten, it's time to get your room updated." I reached up and took down several posters and pennants. "Tomorrow we'll go to the store and buy you some rock music posters. Got any favorite bands?"

"No."

"Then we'll listen to a bunch of music on the Internet until you find one or two. Would you like a poster of a supermodel in a bathing suit or a calendar of them? It's kind of a gross thing that most teenage boys have."

"I guess that's okay."

"Good."

I went to the shelves and pulled off several of the most poorly made airplanes and put them on Donald's lap. "Next we'll get you some new hobbies. Hmmm. Maybe a book or two would be nice. We could get you some games like chess or checkers. Let's think about some video games too."

"Too fast for me," Donald said.

I wasn't sure whether he meant the video games or my whirlwind approach to changing his lifestyle. "You'll learn," I replied.

Next I went to his desk. I picked up the faded flags and raised an eyebrow. "Really, Donald? How long have you had these things?"

"Since we went to Washington, DC."

"That was eight years ago."

"I know. I like them."

I shook my head. "No more. Your desk needs high school-type stuff on it. A calculator, a pen holder, a desk calendar maybe with cool cartoons on it. And these . . ." I motioned to the change counter. "Let's get some money rollers and find out how much you have stashed away here. You could be rich and not know it. Take it to the bank."

Donald only nodded as I cleared his walls and shelves, leaving behind dust prints and pieces of cloudy tape. He made no effort to help or stop me. When I finished, I put my hands on my hips and nodded.

"It already looks better. Don't you think so?"

"No," he answered honestly.

I sat down on the bed next to him and put my arm around his shoulders, giving him a little squeeze. He shrank away from my touch, like usual. "C'mon. Try to imagine how cool it's going to be in here." Donald didn't answer. I guessed he couldn't imagine it at all. So I said, "We'll get you to be the most awesome teenager around. Just agree with me on a couple of things. No more weird noises."

"Okay."

"No more playing kid games."

"Okay."

"We'll go shopping tomorrow."

"Okay."

Satisfied, I left Donald's room and went to my own room to listen to music and write in my diary. I wanted to have a brother like everyone else's.

The next morning, I went up to Donald's room to fetch him for our outing. "Are you ready?"

Donald stood in the middle of his bedroom. His flags, planes, posters, and banners were all back where they'd been the night before.

"Uh . . . yeah," Donald stammered. He snapped his fingers nervously and looked out the window to the front yard. "The Kings play today. It's on at 1:00."

That was Donald's way of telling me that he'd much rather do anything other than what I'd planned for him.

I picked up a roll of masking tape from his desk, ripped off a piece, and rolled it into a little sticky ball. I put the tape on the corner of a pennant that was flapping and pressed it tightly to the wall. Without taking my eyes from the pennant, I asked my brother, "Are you always going to be this way?"

"What way?"

I faced him and noticed immediately how relaxed he was compared to the night before, now that he was surrounded by all his familiar things again. "Stuck, Donald. That's what I mean. It's like you're stuck at age nine or ten."

"I'm sixteen."

"Then you should act like it!"

I couldn't take his questioning expression or the way he just stared at me like I was the crazy one.

"Forget it," I mumbled. "It was stupid of me to try to change you. I don't know what I was thinking."

I slunk out of his room, down the stairs, and out the garage door. Feeling guilty as all get-out, I took a bike ride anyway. I went to the shopping center and looked at CDs and books. It would've been more fun to go shopping with Cathy, but I couldn't call Cathy anymore. It would've been fun to go with Kirk, but he turned out to be a bummer. It might have even been fun to go with Donald, but I'd scared him. Who knew when he would feel comfortable playing with me again?

I missed my old friend, Bobby, more than ever. He never had a problem with Donald when he came over to play, and he often joined us at the park. I remembered how he had a way of teasing Donald that was lighthearted and made Donald laugh. When he picked on Donald, it came out witty and fun-spirited, not mean and harsh like the way I sounded. If Bobby knew about the dumb makeover I'd just tried on Donald's room, he'd give me a hard time about it for hours yet still have a way of making me feel better. That night before bed, I wrote Bobby a long letter about what was going on in my life lately, hoping he'd send me back something to cheer me up. I spent so much time on it that I forgot to study for my spelling test.

10

Not Like My Brother

"And the last word is influential. I-n-f-l-u-e-n-t-i-a-l," spelled Ms. Overstreet. "Now mark the papers. Fewer than two incorrect gets an A. Two to five incorrect gets a B. Six to eight incorrect gets a C. Nine or ten incorrect gets a D. And if you got between eleven and fifteen incorrect, you have to take the test again."

I glanced over at Mark in the desk next to mine. Everyone in the class had to swap their test with someone else for grading, and Mark had mine. He sure had used his pencil a lot. How many did I get wrong?

"Pass them up front, please."

Everyone handed their corrected papers over each other's shoulders until they were within easy reach of Ms. Overstreet's hands. "Mark?" she asked, looking pointedly at the only kid in class who hadn't passed up a test yet.

"Just a second," Mark said. "I'm still counting mistakes."

I dropped my head on the cold desktop.

"Whose are you correcting, Mark?" asked Stacy.

"That's none of your business," Ms. Overstreet reprimanded.

At last, Mark finished and passed it forward. It went past four sets of eyes before reaching Ms. Overstreet. As a teacher, she could have gone to Mark and taken it, knowing everyone was curious. She could have thought about sparing the feelings of the person who'd done so dismally on the test. Apparently, she didn't think that courtesy was necessary. Too bad since one of those sets of eyes belonged to Jackie.

"It's Heidi's," Jackie whispered loudly so everyone could hear as Ms. Overstreet walked back to her desk.

"Figures," said LaQuita.

"Yeah," Kirk agreed.

I raised my head. "What do you mean, 'figures'? What figures?"

"Everyone knows you're a Special Ed-head," Jackie said.

"I'm not in Special Ed," I shot back. "I get really good grades most of the time."

"Sure you do." Stacy rolled her eyes, and the rest of the class laughed.

"There's too much noise in here," Ms. Overstreet said, looking up from the tests. The laughter stopped but only long enough for Ms. Overstreet to say, "Heidi, what happened here?" She waved the test paper near her face like it was a fan.

"I just didn't get a chance to study this weekend is all. I had a lot of stuff to do at home."

The laughter began again. Nasty whispers joined in. "Brain-damaged."

"No. Dame Bramaged. Ha ha!"

"Totally retarded."

Even Cathy had something to say. "I told you."

"You were right."

That was Jackie.

I raised my hand.

"Yes, Heidi," said Ms. Overstreet, who seemed oblivious to all the talking.

"I don't feel well," I said. "Can I go to the nurse?"

"Do you have a fever? You look flushed."

"I just need to go home."

"Have the nurse take your temperature."

I left the insults and went to the nurse's office. Because I didn't have a fever, the nurse wouldn't let me go home. Still, I pretended to be really dizzy when the nurse had me stand up, so I didn't have to go back to class for another hour while I "rested." That was well after lunch.

P.E. that afternoon was highly unusual for me. I got picked last during line-up. Last. After the kids who stank at sports had been picked. And we were playing soccer. My absolute best sport. Didn't anyone remember that I'd won a pin for excellence?

It was Kirk, of all people, who was the team captain who wound up with me on his team. "Man," he whined to Tom. "You know the Program kids reek at sports."

I bit my lip. It was hard not to tell him off, but I decided that it would be better just to show him. Show them all. I could whip the pants off anyone in my class at soccer—even the boys. They were about to see it.

I chose not to pass very much during the game, like I normally would. I was afraid that if I passed the ball, I wouldn't get it volleyed back to me. So I dribbled it through the grass with all my might, dodging classmates to my best ability. Sometimes I took chances that weren't likely to pay off. Still, I made three goals within the first ten minutes or so, enough goals for my team that some of the kids in the class began rooting for me—at least those who didn't care so much about what the inner circle said about me.

Then came a moment I couldn't pass up. Jackie had the ball. She wasn't only popular for her ability to manipulate everyone she met. She was a tall girl, taller than most were at our age. She could really run too. As halfback, I backed way up until I mingled with the fullbacks and let Jackie plow down the field toward me.

I knew her pattern. We'd been playing this game every Monday since the school year began, so I'd gotten to know everyone's strategies. Jackie could run, but she would slow down to shoot. That would be my chance.

Slow. Slow. Bam! I ran up and kicked the ball right between her feet. Rubber soles squeaked as they collided with Jackie's high-top boots. She fell without even having

68

been tripped by me. Legal or no, I could hear Jackie screaming at me as she pulled herself off the ground. I didn't stop to listen. I ran after her ball, snaking it away from anyone who approached. Stacy and LaQuita, who normally stood near the side of the field where the action rarely passed, ran into the fray. The three of them—Stacy, LaQuita, and Jackie—wanted more than the ball.

"Pass it to me!" I heard someone calling to me.

To the side of me, I could see that Kirk had a clear shot to the goal. With Jackie moving in fast, it made the most sense to pass. It was just that I didn't want to pass to Kirk.

Anyone else?

Cathy was in the clear too, but I doubted that she could make the goal to save her life. Best to just try it myself. I slid into the ball and aimed it for the goal.

The ball left my foot, but I didn't watch to see where it went. Jackie's foot collided with my skidding thighs, tripping me while causing a searing pain to shoot up my right leg. From the grass, I looked up. Jackie was pulling herself to her feet. Mud and grass stains streaked her designer skirt and matching vest. A sly smile crossed her face, though.

Over at the goal, I saw the ball firmly in the hands of the goalie.

"Man," Kirk groaned to me. "You're so stupid."

Ms. Overstreet blew the whistle to get everyone to line up. I followed the class to the double lines by their classroom door. My whole body ached. I didn't think I'd ever played so hard in my life. Plus I had this enormous, throbbing pain in my thigh from where Jackie had kicked me. Still catching my breath, I heard Cathy's voice just in front of me.

"Hide, you shouldn't have tripped Jackie."

"I didn't do it on purpose."

"That's not what she thinks."

I brushed a sweaty string of hair out of my face. "I guess I don't care what she thinks."

"You should."

"Why?"

Cathy fidgeted a little as if she were tattling. "She's not inviting you to her party."

"Oh! Like I'm surprised."

"And I think she's planning on getting you back."

"Cathy," I said in all seriousness, "I don't care what Jackie does. I know you all think I'm stupid now, but I'm not. In my opinion, you're the stupid one for hanging out with her. And Jackie's stupid because she's too busy caring about herself to notice that she might be wrong once in a while."

Cathy shook her head at me. "I don't know why I bothered to say anything to you at all."

"Neither do I."

I turned my back to Cathy and looked out at the empty schoolyard until Ms. Overstreet ushered us inside. The day was almost over. A couple more nasty notes and some name-calling at the bike racks, and that would be that. *I can handle it*, I kept thinking over and over. *I can handle anything they give me.*

But the next day I stayed home sick.

11

Hiding

My mom walked into my dark bedroom and sat by my feet.

"Ms. Overstreet just called. She's concerned that you've missed so many days of school." She massaged my feet through the blanket. "Frankly, I'm pretty concerned myself. It's been three days now. Do you want to tell me what's wrong?"

"I just don't feel well. I'll be better next week."

"You don't want to go to school tomorrow either? It's Friday."

I shook my head. Definitely not Friday. There was always extra free time on Friday afternoons. More time for my classmates to say and do whatever they wanted. "I just need one more day. That's all."

"Enough to get you to the weekend, huh?" Mom grinned, but her eyes were full of skepticism.

"No, Mom," I shot back. "That's not it."

"Do you need to see a doctor?" my mom asked, suddenly serious.

"I just want to be left alone."

I turned over on my side, away from my mom. I'd barely gotten out of bed since Tuesday morning, partly to keep up the sick act and partly because I was so depressed that I didn't feel like doing anything but lie there with the shades pulled, reading books.

After a minute or so, my mother finally left the room. I wished that the television was in my room so I could flip on some cartoons. Having just snubbed my mom, it probably wasn't the best time to go downstairs and turn on the tube. I leaned over and peeked out the window shades. Donald was walking his bike down the street toward the house. He wasn't making any loud noises. What was up?

I got out of bed and threw on some sweatpants to go with the sweatshirt I'd been wearing in bed. By the time I was dressed, Donald had come in the garage door.

"Oh, my . . . Donald! What happened?" I heard my mom cry in alarm.

"I think I rode my bike in front of someone's car," he stammered.

"You *think*?" our mom questioned. "Did you or didn't you?"

By this time I'd run down the stairs to see for myself. Donald was bruised up, with cuts all over his arms. His khaki slacks and cotton shirt had grease stains and large rips. I gasped at the sight.

"Well . . ." Donald seemed uncertain about how to answer Mom's question. "I know that they got out of the car and *said* I rode in front of them."

"It was Matt and Daryl, huh Donald?" I clarified.

"Uh, yeah. Them and some others."

"Mom, those are the guys who were following me around on Saturday." She nodded her understanding. I faced my brother. "Did they beat you up?"

"They, uh, they said I was in their way."

"Were you?" I pushed.

"I guess so. That's what they said."

"Come on, Donald," I said, getting angry. "Don't be a wimp. Either you were in their way or not. Did they have any reason to beat you up?"

"Heidi," my mom warned, knowing I was pushing him too hard.

"I . . . I . . ." Donald began to break down. Forehead creased, strained smile. I knew the expression well.

"You're so pathetic!"

I stormed back upstairs and slammed the door.

My mom hollered after me. "Heidi, get back here!" I didn't respond. I didn't care what my mom thought of me right then. If Donald was going to let bullies beat him to death, let him. I wasn't going to protect him anymore since no one bothered to protect me.

Fifteen minutes later (I guess it took that long because my mom had to help Donald clean up all his scratches), my mom walked into my room and closed the door behind her.

"What has gotten into you? What you said to Donald was completely unfair."

"So?"

"How would you feel if you were the one who was beaten up today?"

"And what makes you think I wasn't?"

"What do you mean?"

I turned over and buried my face in my pillow. "Nothing," I said, but it was muffled by the cotton fluff.

"Are you having trouble with your friends at school?"

I shrugged and sat up, punching the pillow as I spoke. "Friends? I don't have any friends thanks to the freak of a brother I have. No. I have a bunch of kids at school who are planning to play some kind of trick on me tomorrow night because they think I'm a retard like Donald."

"Heidi," my mom warned, "we don't use that word."

"Oh, yeah," I said nastily. "I forgot. I just hear it said to Donald and me so often that I forget it's not a compliment."

My mom sighed. "I know it's hard growing up with a brother like Donald, but you can't take your anger out on him. He can't help it."

"I know," I said. "I just wish that for once he would fight back. Daryl and Matt shouldn't be allowed to pick on him like that and get away with it. Why can't he toughen up?"

"You think it would be better if Donald fought those boys?" Mom asked.

"I guess. I don't know."

"If he tried, we would be at the hospital with him now. Is that what you want?"

"No." I pulled my hair over my eyes. "I just want things to be normal."

Mom smiled softly and snuggled me under her arm. "We just have to redefine normal in this house." Then she brushed the strands back out of my face so she could see my eyes. "I have an idea. Since you need a punishment for being so rude to your brother and you need an excuse not to be home when your friends come tramping by to bother you, how about you help out at your brother's dance tomorrow night?"

I moaned. "Do I have to?"

A night surrounded by Donalds trying to dance sounded horrendous.

"Yes, you have to." My mom smiled a mom smile. "In return, I'll let you stay home from school tomorrow even though you're not really sick."

"Are you going to tell Ms. Overstreet?"

"I'm not sure what I'll tell her right now, but you don't have to worry about it." She stood up. "Okay? Tomorrow night is set."

"Great. Can't wait," I said not even attempting to sound enthusiastic.

"Don't fret. You might actually have fun. Plus, there will be pizza and lots of junk food."

My mom exited, leaving the door open. As I got up to close it, I saw Donald limp down the hall from the bathroom to his bedroom. I followed him and tapped lightly at his door.

"Who's there?" Donald asked.

I was about to say, "Who do you think?" but checked my sarcasm. He wouldn't understand it and didn't deserve it. "It's me."

"Oh, hi, Heidi," he said. "I'm drawing pictures of snake monsters. Want to see?"

I went into his room and picked up one of his pictures, a messy ink drawing on ruled notebook paper. "Cool," I said with forced enthusiasm. "It's got big fangs. Are you going to make a story to go with it?"

"Yeah, I guess."

He started drawing a new picture. I watched him as he drew in the same spot over and over again. From habit, I started directing him.

"Put something over here," I said, pointing to an empty spot on the page. "His tail or something."

"Okay." Donald followed my advice and then started to get stuck at that spot too.

"I'm sorry for yelling at you earlier," I said.

"That's okay," he said, his eyes staying entirely focused on his ever-darkening picture.

"Is there anything you can do about those guys? Tell someone at school or something?"

"I think I'll just stay away from them."

I looked at his new picture. It had turned into a two-headed snake with one tail. "Look, it's them." I pointed to each head. "Daryl and Matt."

Donald laughed. He got the joke. "Maybe I'll make up a story about how I'm a great wizard, and I use my magic to change them into these snakes," he said.

"Sounds good," I said. "And they're so busy yelling and being mean that they can never agree on which way to go and wind up stuck on both sides of a cactus."

"Brrrh-hooo!" Donald cheered.

As a favor, I did the actual writing while Donald made up the words. He couldn't spell that well, and his handwriting was illegible. We brought our illustrated story down at dinnertime and read it to our parents. It wasn't a great story, but they seemed so tickled that we had created something together and that the tension of the day was finally over that they laughed all the way through it.

12

At the Dance

The dance was in the largest party room at the bowling alley. When lanes freed up, people left to have a turn at bowling. No one was dancing. The music was the same as what was playing in the whole bowling alley, so aside from streamers and a disco ball hanging from the ceiling, it didn't look much like a dance.

Donald had been part of a club for people from the Life Skills classes since he entered high school, and this was their regular meeting place once a month. The dance was designed to raise money for the club so that they could go on a camping trip to Catalina Island. Some of the members in this group had much severer disabilities than Donald. I saw a couple of wheelchairs and one girl using a walker. I don't know what all else was required for these kids to be safe and healthy, but I assumed that a trip as big as traveling on a boat to an island and then camping overnight would need quite a few adult volunteers and probably a number of paid staff as well. Based on the small attendance, I had a feeling this dance was not going to raise enough money for all that. Hopefully they had some other ideas in mind.

After meeting all the teachers and assistants who helped Donald and his friends with their work at school, I thought I might like to go on that trip, too, to help out in some way. My mom had been right. I was having a pretty good time, mostly because in this setting Donald was one of the highest functioning people there. It wasn't possible for me to be embarrassed by him.

Due to the fact that everyone in the group was so different from each other, I was desperate to know which disabilities Donald's friends had. My mom told me I wasn't allowed to ask that. She said it was rude. "Just talk to everyone like they're no different from you or me."

"But Mom, I just want to know the condition—"

"I'll make you sit outside on a bench all evening if I hear you asking anyone," she said. Dad backed her up with some extra warnings of his own.

I thought they were being pretty ridiculous, and the questions burned on my tongue all evening with each person I met. Donald's best friend (whom I didn't know existed) was a guy named Peter. Even though he had the ability to recite the first five pages of *The Hobbit* by heart, I had to walk this hulking, six-foot-three boy to the bathroom because he couldn't understand the directions. I also had to keep him from biting his left hand, which was permanently scarred from his front teeth. What kind of disability was that? Was it like Donald's but way more intense?

Then there was this other boy named Kincaid. He was on the small side, almost as short as me, so I took him to be a freshman. This boy twitched, barked, and swore alternately, particularly when he got nervous. What caused a person to do that? I met a few kids who looked like some characters I'd seen on TV. Their faces were round and their eyes small. One of them, a girl named Kathryn, was very cheerful and was excited about the e-reader she recently got for her birthday. In a thick voice that was sometimes hard to understand, she told me several times that she could enjoy all the popular books now because she could make the font big enough to read.

When I knew my mom wasn't in earshot, I asked her, "Do you have trouble reading because of your. . .?" I let it dangle on purpose, hoping she'd finish my sentence for me.

"Oh, yes," she said, nodding enthusiastically. "My Down Syndrome makes my eyes have trouble." She pointed at another girl who was walking by. "Claire has a hard time reading, too, but that's because she's mentally retarded."

"Wait. You actually called her 'retarded'?" I whispered the last word, afraid to say it all the way out loud. It didn't matter, though. Claire heard us anyway.

Claire stopped in her tracks and began to shout at Kathryn and me. "I'm not retarded! I'm not! Shut up, Kathryn! I don't like that!"

Ms. Anderson, my brother's Life Skills teacher, rushed over to us, put her hands on Claire's shoulders, and led her out of the party room. Kathryn and I followed her out to the main lobby where we found Ms. Anderson saying some quiet, soothing words near Claire's ear. It took a minute to calm her down because Claire kept shouting things like, "She's not supposed to say that! You said she couldn't say that!"

Their teacher said some more things that I couldn't hear over the music playing, but after a moment Claire quit raging and lifted her tear-streaked face to Kathryn. "Say you're sorry."

"I'm sorry," Kathryn said easily enough. "Want to go bowl?"

Then they took hands and strolled away together like nothing happened.

I imagined going up to Cathy and ordering her to say she was sorry for blabbing about my brother to Jackie and the others and ruining my life. How awesome would it be if she just did it and then we wandered off from the other girls at recess to play handball and laugh with each other like old times?

Ms. Anderson was about to walk away, and that snapped me out of my ridiculous daydream. I skipped up beside her and touched her shoulder to get her attention. "Why did Kathryn call that girl retarded? Isn't that a bad word?"

Ms. Anderson smiled gently at me. The lines around her eyes deepened in a way that let me know she smiled more than she frowned. I would think her life would be very hard working with these special needs teenagers all the time, but her bright eyes and laugh lines suggested otherwise. "We're all pretty sensitive about that word being used incorrectly. There is, in fact, a condition that goes by that name, but we prefer to say 'developmentally disabled' or 'developmental delayed'. A little more eloquent, don't you think?"

I liked the way she spoke to me in a light voice that made her words very clear but didn't make me feel like she was treating me like I was a baby. How long did it take her to perfect that style of speaking? I wondered whether that was how she talked to my brother and his friends. It would be hard to talk to them like normal teenagers, wouldn't it? So many of them sounded like little kids.

I agreed. "My mom said I couldn't ask about what's wrong with everyone here."

She winced. "We're also pretty sensitive about saying something's 'wrong' with our friends here."

"Oh. Sorry."

"Look, I see that you're interested in learning something, but I can't go into specifics about everyone's different diagnosis. There are confidentiality laws . . ."

"I understand," I told her.

Right then I heard a cheer from one of the bowling lanes. I followed the sound to find Donald, Peter, and two other boys cheering about someone's score with their arms raised over their heads. Donald and Peter did an awkward high five. I wondered what the score could be.

"Great job, Donald!" Ms. Anderson shouted.

"Donald?"

I guess the shock in my voice came out a little more than I expected because Ms. Anderson patted me on the shoulder and said, "Your brother is a pretty good bowler. The best in the group by far."

"Really?" I could hardly believe it. My awkward brother? "I can barely pick up a bowling ball, let alone score well."

"Donald just might surprise you sometimes, I think."

"Ms. Anderson?" I bit my lip and then blurted it out. "I know you can't talk about the other kids in your program, but can you tell me about Donald? He's my brother and all, and I would love to know more about why he's, you know, the way he is."

Ms. Anderson sat down with me by the concession stand and took the time to explain to me how Donald had a combination of disabilities. She said he was on the higher end of the Autism Spectrum. Along with that he had poor eyesight and Attention Deficit Hyperactivity Disorder. That made him, in simple terms, slow to understand things and mature.

"Do my parents know all this about him?"

"Yes. We have meetings a couple times a year to discuss how he's doing and make goals for him."

I focused on the group around my brother's bowling match. My mom and dad sat at a table behind them, cheering for him like he was a five-year-old in a T-ball game. "Why have my parents never told me about his condition?"

Ms. Anderson gave a tiny shrug and offered, "I couldn't say. Perhaps they didn't think you were ready to hear it?"

All those times I got in trouble for yelling or making fun of Donald, doing mean things like locking him out of the house or just being impatient with him—I hadn't exactly been proving myself to be very mature. No wonder my parents thought I wasn't old enough to handle this kind of information. I was grateful that Ms. Anderson was giving me this chance to understand.

"Will he always be like this?"

That was the big question.

"Yes, he will," Ms. Anderson said, raising her eyes to watch Donald and his friends. "We'll help him get a job before he graduates from high school, and maybe someday he'll be able to live on his own. But he'll always be Autistic and will always need someone to watch over him and help him out with things."

"As long as he lives? His whole life?"

Ms. Anderson nodded and patted me on the knee. "You're a good sister, Heidi. Donald is very lucky," she said. Then she walked away from me to go check on how everyone was doing. I sat there a few minutes longer, thinking over everything the teacher had told me. I didn't feel like I was a good sister. I felt mean and hateful. Mostly, I felt really trapped.

13

A Surprising Night

I sat there for a while just staring at my hands, trying to understand everything that Ms. Anderson had told me. I must've been pretty lost in my thoughts because I didn't notice that my dad had sat down beside me until he took one of my hands into his own. "What are you doing by yourself?"

I wasn't sure what to say, so I mumbled, "Nothing. I'm just bored, I guess."

"They need some help with the snacks," he said. "Would you like to do that?"

"Sure."

He led me to the party room. It had gotten steamy hot in there over the past hour. That explained why all of the partiers had left the room to go bowling or play arcade games. Against one wall was a table full of cookies, cake, punch, and soda. Ms. Julia, one of the teaching assistants, stood behind the table looking a little frazzled. Her stringy brown hair was up in a messy ponytail, with strands hanging down and stuck to her neck with sweat. The front of her t-shirt and jeans were sopping wet, and her hands were stuffed with punch-stained napkins.

"Do you need some help?" I asked her.

"I could use a break," she said. She wiped her forehead, but it left a streak of cherry-colored punch there. "Do you mind helping out for a bit?"

"She would love to," my dad answered for me.

Ms. Julia scooted out from behind the table and dropped her napkins on the over-stuffed trashcan where they tumbled off and to the floor. She reached out to hug me, but I backed away. That made her laugh as she looked down at her sticky hands. "Thank you so much! You're saving my life!"

While my dad and I cleaned up the spilled punch and got the snacks back in order, I chewed on my lip, trying to figure out how to phrase what I wanted to ask him.

"Just blurt it out," he finally told me. I guess it was pretty obvious I had something on my mind.

I took a breath and started in. "Ms. Anderson said that Donald was going to need someone to help him his whole life." I paused, kind of afraid of the words forming in my brain. I lifted my eyes to his. "What happens when you and Mom are gone? When you can't take care of him anymore?"

"That's a big subject," he said to me. He took the paper cups out of my hand and put his arms around me for a hug. "Your mom and I plan to be around for a long, long time."

"I mean, I know you're not . . . But someday . . . Donald is a lot younger than you . . ."

He continued to hold me, my face pressed against his chest. "Years and years from now, hopefully at least forty or more, when you're all grown up and we've finally gone, we'll have a plan in place for your brother's care."

My stomach clenched. Mrs. Anderson wasn't kidding. Donald's disabilities were life-long. He'd need someone to be helping him even when he was an old man. Here I'd been spending all my time freaking out about how I was going to get through junior high and high school without being embarrassed by my brother. Picturing Donald and myself as old people was too hard for me to grasp.

My dad lifted my face with his finger and looked me in the eyes. "Don't worry your head about this now, sweetie. We've got plenty of time. Life is long, and when changes come, it'll be okay."

Would it?

Dad gestured to the snack table. "Can you handle this for a little while?"

"I got it. Yeah." Dad kissed me on the forehead and went back out to join my mom and the bowling lanes.

Taking charge of the snack table was a great distraction because the students and staff stopped by constantly to get treats. My job was to pour sodas or punch for people who needed help and to put plates of goodies together so no one would have to take a lot of time making decisions about what to eat. This was also a great job because I got to sneak a lot of snacks for myself.

Kathryn and Claire came in after I'd been in there about twenty minutes, giggling so hard at each other that I could barely understand what they were saying. Something about a boy that was "so hot!" Kathryn kept blushing and covering her face with her hands. Happy feelings bubbled up inside of me at the sight of them, and I wanted to be included in their joy.

"Who is it?" I asked.

Kathryn turned to me and, with the biggest grin I've ever seen, shouted, "This boy! Oh, my goodness!"

Claire jumped up and down a hundred times while shouting, "He asked me to dance with him!"

"Well, if you're that excited about it, why aren't we dancing?" came a boy's voice from the door. "You just ran off."

"Oh, my goodness!" Claire squealed. I've never seen someone turn redder in the face. She grabbed Kathryn's hand and ran past the boy out to the bowling alley, squealing some more.

"There she goes again." The boy watched the two girls run away. I watched him. He leaned so casually against the door frame. He wasn't tall, but his reddish-brown hair was soft and long on top, probably giving him an extra inch. His face was freckled, and he sported a mouthful of braces. Even so, he was really cute. I could see why the girls were gushing over him. He turned his face fully toward me, and I felt the color in my own face deepen.

"Hi, I'm Russell," he said, stepping up to the table and snatching a chocolate chip cookie off one of the plates. If Russell was in high school, then whatever his disability was made him look really young. From all appearances Russell looked my age or maybe just a touch older.

"I'm Heidi," I responded. "You're supposed to take the whole plate."

"Oh." Russell picked up the plate and balanced it on one hand while he picked through the goodies with his other. I had seen people struggling all evening with that very same task, and he did it as if it were nothing. I wondered what his disability could be.

"Um," Russell said, holding up a vanilla wafer, "I don't care for these. Can I trade you for another of those pink frosted ones?"

"I guess so," I said with more amazement in my voice than I wanted to reveal. He was so good with words. So clear. I handed him the cookie he wanted. "I like those frosted ones too. I think I sneaked most of them out of the bag already. You're lucky you got one at all."

Russell laughed and held the cookie out for me. "You can keep it if you want. My gift to the hard-working."

"It's all right." I blushed and waved the cookie away.

He munched it down in one bite.

"You don't know how to eat cookies right," I said. "You boys all swallow sweets. You need to enjoy the taste." I picked up the last frosted cookie. "Watch and learn," I said and ate a small bite of it, tilting my head back to catch any crumbs that might break loose, chewing it slowly and letting each bit of the sugar affect my taste buds before swallowing. It took three bites like to finish the one-inch delicacy. "See?"

"That's really something," he said. "Too bad there aren't any good cookies left to practice with." He popped a whole Oreo into his mouth, chewed, and swallowed. Then he looked at me and spread his hands defensively. "What? I suppose you're the break-it-apart-and-eat-the-middle-first kind of gal."

"No," I said. "I'm a dunker."

"Will you use any drink or just milk?"

"Just milk," I said. "Or coffee."

"Eww! You drink coffee?" He made the most awful face.

"Aw, it's not so bad," I said. "You should try it."

"I have. It smells better than it tastes. Like popcorn."

I frowned playfully. "Don't be putting down popcorn."

"Never," Russell returned. "I couldn't see a movie without it. I'm just saying that it smells wonderful, but the taste is always a disappointment."

"I guess I'll have to agree with you."

Russell glanced out the door where someone was waving for him to come over. "Oh, my lane is open. I gotta go."

"Oh." I wanted him to stay. "Well, I'm like the bartender tonight, so if you want anything, you know where to find me."

Russell smiled, revealing a charming dimple in his left cheek, and dumped his plate in the trashcan. He started to walk away.

"Hey, Russell," I called after him. "Where do you go to school?"

"Franklin Junior High. I'm in seventh grade, and my brother is one of your brother's best friends." He saluted me. "Bet you didn't know any of that, did you?"

"No," I admitted. "You're way ahead of me."

"Maybe after my game, which I'll no doubt win, we can talk more about what you like to eat at the movies."

I grinned unashamedly. "Sounds good to me."

Later that evening Russell brought his brother over, a guy named Alex. He didn't look like he had any problems like Donald, but the way his eyes never stopped moving and he kept looking over his shoulder clued me in to the meaning of short attention span. I didn't tell him that Donald had never mentioned him because it seemed very clear from the way he talked that Alex really valued their friendship. It was decided that Alex, Donald, Russell, and I would all go to the movies—at a new movie theater —the following weekend.

After the dance, I was in a daze as I rode home with my family. Who would have thought that I would meet the perfect boy at an event like that?

I was so busy daydreaming about Russell that I didn't hear my father shout. Only my mom's agitated response came through my haze.

"I don't know, honey! Heidi said the kids at school were planning a trick."

I looked out the car window. Our house was covered in toilet paper. Not only draped with it, but someone had hosed it down with water so that it would be even harder to clean up. My stomach flipped, and all the cookies and punch threatened to rise up.

"Oh, no," I moaned.

"Oh, no is right," Dad growled. "What kind of kids would do this? First Donald gets beat up, and now this?" Dad pulled into the paper-lined driveway and stopped the car. He smacked the steering wheel. "We should call the police."

"Oh, honey," my mom said. "It's just a prank."

"And those kids beating Donald yesterday? Was that a prank? Some sort of joke?"

"No," Mom said quietly.

"Well, I'm sick of this!" Dad shouted. He jammed his finger so hard into the remote to open the garage door that I was surprised it didn't break. With the engine still running, he put his hand on Mom's headrest and twisted around to look at me. "Do you know who did this?"

"I have an idea, but I don't know for sure."

"We're going to call their parents," he said to my mom.

That sick feeling worsened. "No, Dad! Please! That'll make it worse!"

My mom sighed. "Why do you kids always think it's going to get worse when we talk to other adults about you being bullied? Their parents need to know."

"You don't understand," I told her. "Please let me handle it."

Dad hit the gas to drive the car inside and then hit the brakes so hard that the car screeched on the concrete. Donald immediately got out of the car and walked out to the driveway. He lifted his head and took in the whole scene, his overly large Adam's apple bobbing up and down wildly and that crazy nervous smile of his plastered on his face. He walked over to the mailbox and began pulling the toilet paper off. "Daryl and Matt?" he asked me as I came over to him and took the paper out of his hand.

"Not this time," I said. "These were my bullies."

"You have bullies too?"

Yes, thanks to you. I bit that thought down. It was mean, and he didn't deserve it. Not to mention the fact that

Dad and Mom were in earshot and would probably punish me forever. I nodded at him and noted the sadness in his eyes. Donald showed some sympathy for me. I'd never seen him do that before. Without a word, he started to grab at the toilet paper again, but I took his hand to lead him back to the house. I put my arm around him.

"We'll get it in the morning, Donald. Don't let it ruin this evening for you."

"Okay," Donald said, but he kept wadding up paper anyway as he made his way back up the driveway.

"Not tonight, Donald."

"But . . ." His fingers twitched and snapped. I knew it bothered him to leave the mess like it was, but it was too late at night to start cleaning it up.

"I know. It's a mess," I said to him, fully aware we'd be spending most of Saturday morning tearing that mess down.

"It could be worse," my mom said.

"How?" asked my dad.

"They could have used eggs or broken our windows."

"Oh. Well. I feel so much better now." Dad threw up his hands in defeat and marched through the garage and into the house. I was about to follow him when I noticed something stuck to the front door of the house. I walked over to see it better.

YOU CAN RUN, BUT YOU CAN'T HIDE.

Stuck up there in strips of wet paper. At that point I knew this was only the first of many tricks to come. Something had to be done to stop them, and soon. They were right. I couldn't stay out of school forever. Come Monday morning I'd have to face my enemies, and I needed to have a plan.

Thankfully, a much-needed letter from Bobby was waiting for me in the mailbox.

Dear Heidi,

Sorry everyone's being so mean. Sometimes people get scared of what they don't know, and then they do stupid things to pretend that they're not scared. Kirk doesn't deserve to go out with you, so don't even think about him. Cathy isn't a good friend either. I wish I could be there for you, but you know how it is. All I can say is maybe you can teach them what it's like to be Donald. That might help, you know? And I hope you meet a friend who is cool enough to see how much fun Donald can be. I sure miss playing in the park with you guys. Take it easy, and write soon.

Bobby

I hugged the letter to my chest after reading it several times, grateful that we made a pact to write real letters instead of emails. You can't hold and hug an email. I folded it up carefully and stuck it in a special pocket of my backpack so I'd be able to sneak a peek at it at school for some extra comfort.

My parents helped me clean up the house in the morning. Dad got up on the ladder and pulled down the paper that had reached the roof and tops of the trees. Mom focused on cleaning the windows while I was in charge of the paper all over the grass and bushes. She told Donald he didn't have to help and to stay inside. After an hour, though, she changed her mind and called him to come out and join us. "He's come to the door to check on us at least two dozen times," she told Dad and me. "If he's so eager to part of this, then so be it."

I shook my head at my brother as he came outside with a giddy smile on his face and immediately started gathering up toilet paper. If it were me, I think I'd have stayed inside and watched TV. He's a better person than me.

It didn't take long before Donald and I had turned cleaning into a game. We pretended we were cleaning up after an alien attack, and we wound up having fun. Sadly, there wasn't enough time to go to the park like he wanted to, but in the late afternoon we rode our bikes to the store to get ice cream sandwiches as a treat.

I ate my ice cream and thought about Russell's freckles and Bobby's sweet note, trying to savor this happy moment because I knew Monday morning I'd have to go back to school and face Jackie and her friends.

14

Monday Morning

Mom drove me to school Monday morning. It wasn't necessary, and although we only lived a few blocks from the place, she went way out of her way to go through the drive-thru so she could get me some French toast sticks and a hot chocolate—her bribe for making me get up that morning and face the day. The chocolate tasted good on my tongue, but it soured in my stomach the moment I got to school and had to walk through all the teasing laughter and jeering of the kids in school to get to class. Clearly, the news about my house being papered had spread.

All morning while Ms. Overstreet lectured about different kinds of American Indian dwellings that had been constructed around the country based on the terrain, the sweets rolled around in there. I thought I might genuinely have to go home sick if it didn't stop soon.

Ms. Overstreet finally brought her lesson to an end and said it was time to do a fun project. She lit up the way she does when she thinks she's doing something that will get kids all excited about learning. She smiled bigger, her eyes widened, and her hands gestured wildly. Even that dark bob haircut of hers seemed to get animated.

"I want you to split into groups of four. I've got craft materials for each group. You get to create a structure: a teepee, an adobe hut, a pueblo, a wigwam, a longhouse . . . You get to pick, and you get to design it. Sound fun?"

I think one person said yes. I'm pretty sure that was Cathy because she loved crafts. I know for a fact I heard several groans from the boys. I held mine in, but it would have been loudest if I hadn't. I hated crafts *and* the idea of being in a group. All I wanted was to throw up and go lie down somewhere.

At least Ms. Overstreet could have picked the groups for us, but she didn't. She left it up to us to find a few friends. Naturally, no one picked me. I saw Michelle Blanco coming toward me (the only person who did), but Jackie said, "Not her." Michelle changed direction and joined another group. When all the groups were settled, only three of us remained. Myles Tucker, Kimi Belyakov, and myself. Kimi was a Foreign Exchange student and didn't speak English very well. She also had some unfortunate eyebrows and a big mole on her cheek. Myles was a big boy and had an unfortunate body odor. My former friends always kept their distance from these two unless they were in a teasing mood.

I glanced over at Jackie and the girls. By the way they were laughing and pointing, I could tell they were enjoying the fact that I was stuck with the two outcasts of the sixth grade. Over in the corner, Kimi smoothed the top of her hair with her hands and tightened her ponytail. Myles chewed on his nails. Both of them watched me carefully, surely expecting me to come over and say something horrible to them.

I turned my back to Jackie and walked to Kimi and Myles. "Would it be okay if I joined you two?" They both nodded, and we got to work.

It turned out that Myles was a wiz at building, and Kimi had lots of great ideas for making the structure cool-looking. Neither of them seemed to be aware of the hard time the popular kids had been giving me because they were super friendly and talked to me like they thought I was worth their attention. Despite Myles's underarms, my nausea began to abate. I found myself laughing and enjoying their company. We made a pretty awesome building and were finished well before the cut-off time. I looked around and saw several groups panicking about finishing in time. Kirk was yelling at his friends and running his hands through his normally neat hair.

Jackie, Stacy, LaQuita, and Cathy weren't freaking out. They also finished with minutes to spare. That didn't surprise me. Cathy was pretty artistic just by herself, and I was sure the other girls had some talent for decoration. The four of them leaned against their desks, smirking like they thought they were hot stuff while keeping their project hidden behind them.

"All right! Time's up!" Ms. Overstreet announced in her cheery voice. Kids groaned and yelped. "Let's see what everyone made." She held up a cardboard box that was open on the top. "Everyone grab a few scraps of paper from this box. Walk around and look at all the structures. On your paper score each project from one to five and put it in a neat pile to the side of the project. Five means it's perfect. The structure with the highest number of votes wins."

"Wins what?" Jackie asked.

"No homework tonight," Ms. Overstreet said. "How's that?"

"Aw, man," Kirk whined. "If I'd known there was a prize, I'd have worked harder."

Ms. Overstreet raised her eyebrows. "You should always work your hardest, no matter whether there's a prize." She shook the box. "Come on, everyone."

I went to grab some paper for my scores. Most of my classmates chatted with each other about the houses and decided in groups what the scores should be. I kept my thoughts to myself, wrote my score, and slipped my vote under each pile so no one would know it was mine. None of the projects impressed me that much. I truly believed the one Myles, Kimi, and I made was the best. I already had a huge pile of make-up work for the days I missed, so I was pretty thrilled about the idea of not having any new homework to add to it.

I put my final score down on Kirk's group project. It was awful and had already fallen over. I gave it a one. My finger had just left the pile of votes (all of which, I noticed, agreed with my opinion) when I heard a bunch of laughter coming from behind me. I flipped around to see what was going on. Nearly everyone in the class was gathered around the house my group had made. Oh, no! What happened to it? I rushed across the room and pushed my way between my classmates.

Our little, perfect longhouse made of individual clay bricks that Myles, Kimi, and I took care to create was completely covered in shreds of white paper. Some of it had been pressed into the clay, ruining the structure, and other pieces were piled on top.

"It looks just like Heidi's house!" Stacy shrieked, laughing in a way that sounded a lot like a cackle to me. All of the other kids in the class laughed. Except Myles and Kimi. They were devastated and looked at me with painful eyes. Now they knew I wasn't someone they should have teamed up with, but it was too late.

Rage took over. I dashed over to Jackie's project, lifted it up, and threw it across the room. It sailed over three desks and slammed into the bulletin board on the side wall with a bang. The clay stuck to the bulletin board and ripped it off the wall, where the whole thing fell off and plopped to the floor. Push pins, toothpicks, notes, and clay scattered everywhere. I heard a collective "Oh!" from the class, but I refused to look at any of them. My blood felt so hot, and my fingers tingled. I thought I might pass out.

"Heidi Lansing!" Ms. Overstreet shouted at me.

"I . . . I . . ." I didn't know what to say. I slowly pivoted to find the whole class staring at me with their mouths frozen in this "O" shape. No one moved, including my teacher. I thought about apologizing, but right then Jackie started to smile. It was the meanest smile I'd ever seen, and it was directed right at me.

As quickly as it appeared, she wiped it away and began tugging on Ms. Overstreet's sleeve. "Did you see what she did, Ms. Overstreet? She ruined our project!" That got LaQuita and Stacy into action too, and they also started whining about how I ruined all their hard work and must be punished. Cathy continued to stare at me like I was crazy, shaking her head like she couldn't quite believe it.

I ran over to Ms. Overstreet and the girls. The other students in the class backed out of the way. I noticed that Mr. Roland, the teacher from the class next door, was poking his head in the door. He must have heard the bang and wondered what happened. Above it all, I heard the phone ringing.

"They ruined my project first," I shouted. "They put paper all over it and ruined it. They came to my house over the weekend and toilet-papered my house. They deserved it!"

We were all shouting at once.

"Everyone stop!" Ms. Overstreet shouted. We silenced ourselves. None of us had ever heard her so angry before. "Go to your seats." Everyone slunk back to their desks except for the girls and me. "I meant all of you," Ms. Overstreet said to us.

"This is Jackie's fault," I said. "If she hadn't been so mean—"

"My fault? You can't pin anything on me. The whole class saw you throw our longhouse—"

"You ruined mine."

"Oh, please."

"Girls!"

We shut our mouths. Cathy, LaQuita, and Stacy snuck back to their seats.

Ms. Overstreet waved at Mr. Roland. "Could you send Ms. Latham over here to watch my class for a few minutes?" He nodded and left the doorway. We stood there silently until Mr. Roland's assistant came over. Ms. Overstreet gave the class some quick directions about cleaning up the projects and reading until recess. Then she took Jackie and me to the front office.

Our principal, Ms. Hudson, sighed and huffed the whole time we were in her office. She listened to us argue, but she kept flicking her eyes at Ms. Overstreet as if to ask why our teacher was wasting her time with this issue.

"Jackie," she finally said, "from now on, keep your opinions about Heidi and her brother to yourself. It isn't your business or anyone else's. Can you work on that?"

"Yes, ma'am," Jackie said with a nod.

"We have a zero tolerance policy for bullying."

"But I promise I didn't—"

"If I hear about you bothering Heidi again, there will be consequences. Do you understand?"

"Yes, ma'am."

Then Jackie left with Ms. Overstreet to go back to class. Because I'd committed a violent act and ruined school property on top of it, I got in-school suspension. My mom was called, and I had to spend the rest of the day sitting at a small desk behind the administration assistants in the front office. Kimi brought a stack of work and dropped it in front of me. I took her hand to stop her before she left.

"I'm so sorry, Kimi."

She gave me a sympathetic smile. "It is not a worry, Heidi," she said. "I too have not much friends. Sometimes I too get mad."

"I'm sorry if I was ever mean to you."

"You were not. You let me play the game of dodging balls."

"That's right," I said, remembering how hard she could throw the ball. "You were good at it."

"I like that game. We maybe play again sometime?"

"I'd like that."

I hoped that would happen, but I had a feeling it would be hard to get anyone to play with us after what I'd done that morning. If there were kids in the sixth grade who hadn't sided with Jackie in hating me yet, they certainly would now. I was glad I didn't have to go back to class because I didn't know how I'd be able to raise my head enough to look at anyone. The thought of going back the next day made me want to cry. Could I convince my mom to let me change schools?

Another hour passed, and my stomach growled. It was getting close to lunchtime. I raised my head from my work to see a teacher I didn't recognize rolling a really small child into the office in a wheelchair. The kid in the chair didn't even look like she was in kindergarten. Her wrists and ankles were twisted in a way that looked unnatural, and her head tilted to the right. Drool ran out of her open yet smiling mouth. Her black hair was thick and unruly. I watched her get pushed into the nurse's office next to where I was sitting. They left the door open, and I leaned forward to see what they were doing.

Our school nurse, Ms. Wren, greeted the little girl warmly and pulled out a can of some kind of milk from the refrigerator. Ms. Wren and the teacher talked to each other and to the little girl, but the little girl just grunted and giggled. While they chatted, Ms. Wren poured the milk into an IV-type bag and pressed buttons on a square machine next to it. She then attached a long tube from the bag to the little girl's stomach. A beep or two later and the milk was slowly going through the tube into the girl's body.

"Is that how she eats?" I asked them.

Ms. Wren and the teacher looked up, a little surprised to find me watching them. They both explained to me how tube feeding worked and that they had to do this twice a day for her. It took about thirty minutes for all the milk to go through. The whole time I thought about the dance a few nights before and how interesting it had been to learn about Donald's difficulties and meeting his friends. I wondered what it was like for this little girl's brothers or sisters, the fact that she had to eat like this. Could they go to restaurants? Did they get embarrassed to have friends come over for lunch or dinner? Or did they just handle it?

I pulled the letter Bobby had written to me out of my pocket and read it again.

All I can say is maybe you can teach them what it's like to be Donald. That might help, you know?

I let that notion roll around in my head for a little while.

By the time the tube feeding was done and the teacher rolled the little girl back to class, I had an idea. I gently tapped on Ms. Hudson's door and asked whether she had a minute to talk. She took her hand away from her keyboard and sighed at me before waving me inside. Five minutes later, her eyes were bright and she was smiling at me. She patted me on the back and said, "That just might work."

15

What It's Like to Be Special

Right after the first bell had rung for school to start the next morning, Ms. Overstreet had announced that we were going to have a special activity for the day. Ms. Hudson had arranged for the class to volunteer in the Special Education program until lunchtime. A lot of the kids whined because it meant we'd miss recess for the day, but most of the class was okay with it because it also meant no math or social studies. The biggest complaint came from Stacy, who said that if she'd known she was going to have to spend the day with drooling, stupid babies she wouldn't have worn her favorite dress. She had to stay behind in Mr. Roland's class and write 100 sentences about being polite and accepting of others before she was allowed to come join us.

If Jackie, LaQuita, or Cathy had something rude to say, they buttoned their lips up really fast after that. I didn't hear a peep from them as we marched in lines around the school to the primary side of campus. Ms. Overstreet led us through a gate and across the fenced-in play yard that the preschoolers used. Kimi got really tickled about how small the toys were, and Myles made us both laugh when he said he couldn't get his foot in one of the bucket swings, let alone his behind.

Ms. Overstreet hushed us at the door, and with that giddy smile she wore when she thought she was doing something special, she divided our class into four groups of six, one group per Special Education classroom. On purpose, my group consisted of everyone who had been giving me the hardest time: Kirk, Jackie, LaQuita, and Cathy. Stacy would join our group too when she finished writing her sentences. We were sent into the rooms, and Ms. Overstreet said she'd be back to check on us later.

So we stood on one side of the room while the preschoolers sat on the floor in the corner of the room with the teaching assistants. I'd never felt particularly big before, but I felt like a giant next to these little kids.

"I'm Kay," said a tall woman with a blond braid that hung down to the middle of her back. "I'm the lead teacher in this room. These are my teaching assistants, Debbie and Toni." Debbie and Toni smiled and waved at us.

Debbie winked at me; she was the teacher I'd met in the office the day before. She put a hand to the side of her mouth and whispered in my direction, "I think this was a good idea."

I hoped it was, but Debbie might have just ruined it. My plan didn't include letting the other kids in class know it was my idea to spend the day in the school's Early Intervention classrooms. Jackie's eyes darted my way, and her nostrils flared just enough to let me know she wasn't happy. Not one bit. She nudged her friends and nodded her head toward me. Cathy and LaQuita also shot me dirty looks. I purposely didn't respond to Debbie and raised my eyebrows and shoulders a touch to make it appear that what she said was baffling to me.

Kay passed out name tags. "We only go by first names in these classrooms. Our last names are too hard for the little ones to pronounce. Many of our children are just learning to speak or have speech difficulties."

Kirk waved the tag and seemed very confused. "But they can read?"

"Those are for me," Kay said. She waved a hand like she was clearing a cobweb. "We all have a special challenge, really, and mine is that I can't remember names to save my life."

I thought about that as I wrote my name on the tag and stuck it on my shirt. What was my special challenge? I'm horrible with remembering my multiplication tables. I've only passed the tests in class a couple of times, and those were for the multiples of two and five. I watched the other members of the group pat their stickers into place. Did any of them have anything they'd confess was difficult for them? Would any of them admit it?

It was nine o'clock, and according to the schedule on the wall, this was "calendar time." Debbie was overfilling the child-size chair in front of the calendar, helping the preschoolers sing the days of the week. She was probably unaware that her permed hair was blocking Saturday and Sunday. Meanwhile, Toni sat on the floor among the children, staying busy as she used her long, dark fingers with gorgeous fake fingernails to gently nudge faces away from looking at us and back toward the lesson.

"There are only twelve kids in your class," LaQuita pointed out to Kay. "How come you have three teachers?"

Kay nodded at that. "We could really use a fourth teacher to care for these twelve. They're a busy group and need lots of help. That's where you guys will come in handy. Come on over. Sit on the floor between the little ones."

So all of us moved over to the floor and hesitantly picked two tiny tots to sit between.

"Eww!" LaQuita shrieked. "He's drooling!"

"Then get a tissue and help him wipe it up," Kay said in a very no-nonsense tone. "Timothy drools a lot. You have to get used to it."

Toni laughed. "This is a room full of snot, vomit, and drool, girl. It isn't a place for the squeamish."

LaQuita wiped up the drool and dropped the tissue in a nearby trashcan. "I hate this," she whispered to Stacy, who had just arrived and was carefully tucking the folds of her skirt under her legs so the kids couldn't mess it up. Toni placed a tissue box in LaQuita's lap in case she needed more.

Stacy nodded and looked at the kids surrounding her. "Uh, Miss Kay? This little boy is pinching himself like really hard."

"Paul!" Kay said to the boy. He looked up at her, dazed. "Stop pinching. Nice hands." Kay used her hands to accent her words.

"Sign language?" I asked.

"Yes."

"Is he deaf?" Stacy asked, looking Paul over as though she might be able to tell that way.

Debbie answered this one. "We use sign language because these kids haven't learned to verbalize very well yet. Sometimes the signs help put meaning to the words. Many of them will sign before they speak."

I nodded. "I do that with my brother sometimes."

"You would," Kirk said.

I swallowed. This wasn't working. If it didn't start to have an effect soon, this could be a very long day.

The preschoolers had a hard time concentrating on the "Days of the Week" song. Their round eyes traveled to all of the big kids' faces, clearly wondering why we were there. All of us girls had our hair pulled. Kirk wound up with spittle all over his shirt.

A few minutes later the class was split up. Four preschoolers went with each teacher. We sixth graders paired up and sat at the tables with each group. I wound up with Cathy at Ms. Kay's table, where we worked on helping children recognize pictures on flash cards. Jackie and LaQuita went with Toni to do counting skills. I'd like to say they were working with the children, but every time I focused my attention on them, they seemed to have gotten Toni into a big conversation about nails or hair while the preschoolers went mostly ignored. Kirk and Stacy helped Debbie with finger-tracing letters in a tray of sand. That activity looked kind of fun, but Kirk and Stacy seemed more interested in flirting with each other than helping the children. I noticed one of the little tykes was trying to eat the sand at one point and then heard Debbie pick on the two lovebirds for not paying attention.

At our table I was surprised at how involved Cathy got with teaching. She held up each card and said the name of the picture in this really cute, high-pitched voice that I'd never heard her use before. She made it sound like everything she showed them was exciting and interesting. The children responded with energy of their own, even if they didn't always say the right word. By the time we were nearing the end of our last group, Cathy paused and scrunched up her eyes like she was trying to figure something out.

"What is it?" I asked her. I think I expected her to say something about this activity being stupid or pointless, but Cathy didn't answer me.

She turned her focus to Kay. "Some of the kids get the activities easily, and some really don't. They're all different in how they learn, aren't they? Do you know what I'm trying to say?"

"Yes, I know exactly what you mean," said Kay as she held a picture of an orange in front of a little girl. "Carly here can easily put eight little teddy bears on a card with the number eight printed on it, but she has a hard time telling me what this is a picture of."

"Grape," said Carly.

"No," Kay said to her in a gentle voice. "That was the last card I showed you. Try again."

"Grape."

"No." Kay picked up a different card. This one had an apple on it. "What is this?"

"Grape."

To Cathy she said, "See what I mean?" She turned the card to a boy named Paul. "What is this?"

"An apple," Paul said in a strangely monotonous voice, almost robotic.

"Now, Paul here can read at a second grade level, but he can't hold a pair of scissors or draw a straight line."

"That's got to be hard for you as a teacher," Cathy said.

"It's one of the things I like best about this job," Kay confessed. "Every child is a puzzle that I have to solve. And from what I'm seeing, you might be pretty good at solving puzzles yourself."

The tiniest of smiles emerged on Cathy's lips. Her eyes drifted over to me for a second and then dropped back to the cards in her hands.

During snack time, Debbie took the little girl in the wheelchair to the office while Kay and Toni had us help set up for the rest of the children to eat. There were so many directions to follow to keep the children safe that I couldn't imagine how the teachers ever served snacks without six extra helpers.

"Make sure they chew and swallow. Ryan has to have a special drink; he has to drink all of it. Tiffany can't eat anything that isn't mashed up. Don't let . . . Oh! I was going to say don't let Paul push his food off the table. Could you get some paper towels?"

"Definitely," Stacy said, getting away from the spill as quickly as possible.

We cleaned the tables while the teachers helped the preschoolers go to the bathroom. The moment the teachers were out of earshot, Kirk said, "This is so boring!"

"And disgusting!" LaQuita said as she smeared all the mess around on the table with a paper towel. She went to drop her towel in the trashcan, and I cleaned the table up more thoroughly behind her. I noticed that Cathy kept her thoughts to herself as she put all the lunchboxes back in the cubbies.

Stacy stayed to the side of the mess, shaking her hands and jumping up and down like she was completely grossed out. "When is this going to be over?"

Jackie, who had been sitting in a chair backwards, not helping at all, stuck out her hand right as I was passing her to get to the trash can, causing me to slam all of the messy paper towels into my chest. "Is this what your classes were like when you were a retarded baby?" she asked as I picked the ick off of me.

I took a deep breath to control myself. This day had to end well, and it wasn't going to be me who blew it. Not this time. "If you're going to insult me, at least be smart about it," I said coolly. "You and I have been in almost every class together since preschool. Remember?"

Kirk laughed, and Stacy smacked him in the chest. Cathy was smiling full out now. LaQuita sneered at Jackie— not me. Maybe there was some hope.

16

Teaching and Learning

The teachers led the children back into the room, and we all gathered in the corner again for story time. Toni read one picture book and asked if one of us would like to read one. Cathy tentatively raised her hand, and Toni stood and offered her the chair. Little Carly crawled into my lap, and when the other children saw that I let her stay there, some of them tried to crawl in the laps of my classmates. LaQuita smiled hesitantly and allowed a little girl to sit in her lap too. Kirk shrugged and let two preschoolers snuggle close to each side of him and rest their heads against his shoulders. Stacy and Jackie purposely sat on their knees so that the children couldn't sit in their laps. I saw Stacy pick up a girl's hand off her skirt with her index finger and thumb and drop it back in the girl's own lap like it was a dirty rag.

While Cathy read with that same adorable voice she'd used earlier when she was helping Kay with the picture cards, a new teacher entered the room. This woman was dressed more professionally than the preschool teachers, in a skirt and button-up blouse as opposed to a casual shirt and pants.

"This is Renee," said Kay, holding out a hand to present the smart-looking woman. "She's our speech therapist. Many of our students have trouble learning correct pronunciations of words, so Renee works with them one-on-one."

"My brother sees a speech therapist," I said.

"Really?" Renee said. "Who?"

"I think her name is Carolyn Davis."

"Davies," Renee corrected. "She's good. Is your brother in high school then? She only works with older kids."

"Yeah, he's sixteen."

This was the second time I'd mentioned my brother in this environment. My heart raced from the immediate rush of nerves running through me. I tried hard to keep my eyes on Kay and Renee so I wouldn't have to see the reactions from Jackie and my other classmates. I noticed no one said anything rude to me, but then again there were four adults surrounding us at the moment.

Jackie had a question for Renee. "So you're like the expert teacher. The one who really knows how to fix these kids?"

Stacy added, "I guess your job's not as messy since you're wearing nicer clothes."

Jackie's question seemed to fluster Renee, and she acted like she couldn't quite find the words for an answer. Instead she turned her attention to Kay, who had her lips in a tight, thin line as if she was working very hard to hold back what she wanted to say. I totally understood how she felt. After a heartbeat, Kay said, "You're right, we get pretty messy in here, and we're about to get messi-*er*. Time for art!"

Kay whispered something in Renee's ear. Her eyes flicked from Jackie to me as she processed what she'd been told. The speech therapist simply nodded her understanding before taking little Paul's hand and leading him out of the room.

We split up with the children at the three tables again and led them through a simple art project of coloring, cutting, and gluing. The teachers had to keep reminding us not to do the cutting or pasting for the preschoolers.

"The point isn't to make pretty stuff," Debbie explained, removing the scissors from Jackie's hand. "It's to get them to learn how to do these skills." She looked down at the artwork Jackie had been creating with a little girl in a wheelchair and shook her head with disappointment. "Jackie, I'm going to have to start over with this one. It doesn't look like Tiana did it at all."

"Well, she *can't*," Jackie said defensively. "She can't hold the markers or color in the lines. She can't work the scissors. There's no part of this that she can do by herself."

I sneaked a peek at her friends and saw that Stacy, LaQuita, Cathy, and even Kirk were all being very careful not to look at her. LaQuita chewed on her lips as she pointed at spots on the construction paper where little Carly should color with her yellow marker.

Debbie folded up the picture Jackie had made into quarters as she stumbled for the right words to use. Her perky smile had vanished. She looked around the room for something Jackie could do besides helping a child. In a calm, quiet tone, she said, "Maybe you can, I don't know . . . Could you go through our markers and throw out the ones that are dried up? That would be a big help."

Jackie snatched up the box of markers in front of me and yanked one out of my hand before heading toward the counter where the teachers kept their supplies. On her way, she tapped Stacy on the shoulder and motioned that she should come too. Stacy glanced up from where she was helping a little boy named Nick squeeze a glue bottle and shook her head. "Gotta stay here," she whispered. "He needs me to help him or this will be a disaster." She looked down at the paper to find Nick had already created a huge glob of glue.

Stacy put her hands to her face in shock and then started laughing really hard, like she'd lost her mind. All of us, teachers and preschoolers included, stopped what we were doing to watch her. "I totally don't even know how to fix this!" Nick put his fingers in the glue and smeared it around his paper. Then he dropped all the cut-out pieces on it and smashed them into place. Still laughing, she put up a hand, and Nick gave her a sticky high five. "Nick, you're an artist!" Stacy held up the messy picture for everyone to see. "What do you think? Independent enough?" Everyone but Jackie started laughing too.

"Now that's just about perfect," Kay said.

Stacy raised her sticky hands desperately. "Now somebody help *me!*"

At last it was lunchtime for the little ones. Once we got the kids situated outside with the other preschool classes and their lunchboxes, it was time to gather our whole class together again to head back to our side of the school and have our own lunch break. While the teaching assistants stayed outside with the preschoolers, Kay took a moment to field some final questions.

Ms. Overstreet started the questions rolling. "A number of my students have asked me, so I'll let you answer. How does someone become Learning Disabled?"

"Well, first off, we choose not call these children *disabled*. We say they have learning differences or challenges," Kay began. "To answer your question, most of our students are born this way. It can be caused by any number of factors: illness during pregnancy, drug use, or drinking alcohol during pregnancy. It can also be caused by trauma after the birth." Kay paused, and Ms. Overstreet gave the tiniest nod, making me think this question and answer had been planned ahead of time. "It can also be genetic."

"Does that mean it runs in the family?" Kirk asked. I felt the eyes of the whole class on me.

"Kind of," Kay answered, using her hands a bit too much as she spoke to draw the attention back to herself. "There are many things we pass on to our children genetically. For example, a man prone to heart attacks may have kids who grow up to have heart attacks too. Certain kinds of special needs can be like that."

"Can they be cured?" Cathy asked.

"These aren't diseases," Kay said carefully. "They don't have cures. Some cases are mild, and with proper early intervention, which is what we do here, those students might go on to college and great careers. Other kids have it tougher. Still, Special Education students have it much better today than they ever did before."

"Why?" LaQuita asked doubtfully.

"When I was a girl your age, and I'm only forty-eight now, they didn't have programs like this in many schools. I have a sister who has learning differences, but the doctors at the time didn't understand her specific needs. They called her 'brain-damaged.' Sounds nice, doesn't it? Can you imagine calling anyone something horrible like that?"

Some of the kids looked down at their hands. I worked really hard at not looking at any of them accusingly. I took a deep breath through my nose and stayed focused on Kay.

"By the time my sister was in the third grade, the doctors learned a new word. They called her hyperactive. They gave her a lot of medicine to calm her down and told us not to feed her sugar or orange juice. They also pulled her out of the classroom for chunks of the day to meet with a resource teacher. My sister was taught that it was hard to teach her, so she lives at home to this day with my parents and works at a fairly easy job. She can't drive."

She paused to let that sink in.

It was Cathy who spoke up. "What if your sister were a child now? Would it be different? Would she be in a class like this?"

"Absolutely. We would do evaluations and tests to discover that she had Attention Deficit Disorder and a severe hearing impairment. These can be treated. Medication, diet, hearing aids, tutoring, speech therapy, and encouragement could have changed her whole life for the better."

Kay needed to go to lunch or she would miss her break completely, so Ms. Overstreet thanked her for her time and led us back to the other side of the school.

After lunch, the class made thank-you cards for the preschool staff. As we worked, a couple of notes dropped on my desk. I looked up immediately to see LaQuita and Stacy calmly walking back to their desks. Clearly, they didn't care that I knew it was them who dropped the notes. I held the first note in my hand nervously. Heat welled up behind my eyes. I just didn't want to deal with anymore awful things. This field trip to the preschool was supposed to help, and here I was already with another note in my hands. What horrible names were they going to call me now?

I peeked over my shoulder. LaQuita was watching me, but she wasn't giggling behind her hands with Stacy like last time. She gave me a "yes" nod. I wasn't sure what she was trying to tell me. I unfolded the note and read it.

Sorry for being so mean to you because of your brother. —LaQuita

I had to read it twice because I couldn't believe it. Then I opened the other one.

We shouldn't have teased you about your brother. Friends? —Stacy (with a smiley face and a heart)

I felt their eyes on the back of my head, but I couldn't bring myself to look at them again. I wasn't sure whether I believed the sincerity of the notes. I was going to have to give it time to settle in.

A minute later, Cathy stepped up to my desk and tapped her fingers to get my attention. "Heidi, I'm so sorry for being such a jerk. I didn't realize how much of a problem your brother was. That's got to be so hard for you to deal with. I'm sorry for you."

Sorry for me? That sounded worse than the name-calling. I didn't want anyone feeling sorry for me.

"Look," I said in a loud voice that disrupted the whole class. I stood up. "I want to make one thing clear. My brother is not a pity case. He's a pretty cool guy. In fact, he's probably the happiest guy I know and a lot of fun to be around. I don't need your sympathy. What I need is for all of you to leave him and me alone!"

Jackie squinted nastily at me. "Chill out, Hide. You don't have to blow a fuse. We were just apologizing. If you don't want us to, fine." She folded the note she was holding, which I assumed was intended for me, and tucked it into her desk.

"It's not the apology," I said. "It's what the apology is *for* that counts."

The school day ended on that sour note.

17

Someone Gets It Right

"Hold on, Russell," I said into the phone. "I've got another call coming in."

"Okay," he said in his cheery way.

We'd talked on the phone every day since the dance. I found it amazing that we had so much to say to each other even after four days. I wondered whether I could ever run out of things to talk about with someone as neat as him.

I clicked the button. "Hello?"

"It's Kirk," came the familiar voice.

"You don't have to apologize, if that's why you're calling. I won't believe you anyway," I grumbled.

"Just hear me out, okay?" he pressed.

"I have another call waiting," I said, trying to convince him to hang up. After my major failure at school that day, the last thing I wanted was more grief.

"I'll just be a second."

"Okay," I gave in. "What?"

"You were right today in class," he said. "Everyone, mostly me, has been so mean to you and your brother, and it's not cool that we just apologize to you. I mean, Donald should get apologies too, you know. He's probably a good guy once you get to know him."

"He *is* a good guy," I interrupted.

"Yeah, that's what I meant."

"It's not what you said."

Kirk paused and said slowly, "But it's what I meant. Give me a break here." I sighed as he inhaled for his next speech. "I was just wondering whether we could have a second chance. Now that I know what everything's about and all, maybe we could go on that date again."

"I don't think so."

"Why not? I promise not to be such an idiot."

"It's not that," I said. "Well, it *is* that, but also, see, I have a boyfriend now."

"Who?"

"You don't know him. He's in junior high."

"Oh." Kirk was silent.

"I gotta go," I said. "I have a call . . ."

"Oh yeah," Kirk said, pepping up. "Well, if he dumps you, let me know, okay?"

"Sure." There was more awkward silence. Then I broke it when I thought of something. "Hey, Kirk, you know what you *can* do for me?"

"Anything."

"You have a brother on the varsity basketball team at Creek High School, right?"

"Yeah."

"I happen to have a brother who'll be his towel boy for life if your brother will watch out for him and keep a couple of bullies off his case."

I told Kirk all about Matt Tonkovich and Daryl Peck, and Kirk agreed to inform his brother when he got home from practice. Kirk finally hung up.

I clicked back to Russell.

"Well, that took long enough," he teased.

"I hope you don't mind, but I just told someone you're my boyfriend to get him off my back."

"I don't mind."

"Cool."

18

Yes

"Mad aliens are landing on the island!" I shouted up to Donald.

"They're aiming their photon torpedoes right at us!" he shouted back from the crow's nest.

"Then we've only got seconds."

I started to jump over the side, but on second thought I moved back to the stepladder. "Follow me, crewman."

Donald climbed slowly down from the crow's nest and caught up with me on the stepladder. "Do you think we can sneak aboard their spaceship?" he asked.

"No," I said, instinctively, leading him down to the sand. Then I turned to see his disappointed face and corrected myself. "You know what? Yes. Yes! That's a great idea. Let's attack!"

I tightened the knot in the bandanna around my neck and pointed the way. We ran as a team to the top of the strange alien ship and slid into the tunnels. Immediately Russell and his older brother, Alex, came out the bottom and pretended they'd dived into the ocean. Quickly, they "swam" toward the edge of the sandbox with Donald and me in hot pursuit.

"We have phase guns that work underwater!" Russell bluffed.

"No such thing!" I called, aiming for him.

"I've got a harpoon," Alex shouted.

"Whoo-hoo!" Donald shouted as he pretended that the harpoon had jutted through his shoulder. "Help me!"

I "swam" to Donald and tugged at the imaginary harpoon. Russell swam and pulled me off of my brother. We fell backwards into the sand, where Russell immediately cheated by tickling me.

"Stop it!" I cried. "You can't tickle action heroes!"

"I can't?" Russell said, tickling me some more.

Alex went to Donald and pulled out the imaginary harpoon. "I need that for fishing," he said.

"Fishing?" the rest of us questioned.

"Sure," Alex said. "Why not?"

"Yeah," Russell agreed. "Why not?"

126

"Anything goes, right Donald?" I said, slapping my brother's shoulder.

"Brrru-whip!" he agreed.

Author's Note

As a person who was bullied in 6th grade, watched her older brother get bullied because he was differently-abled, and now has supported her daughters through bullying, creating this story was dear to my heart and more personal than any I've ever written.

While this story is fiction, it does pull from experiences my brother and I had growing up. I want to thank my parents and both of my brothers (yes, I have another awesome brother) for being cool and supportive about me writing this novel.

I am thankful to David Kuchta for choosing and editing *No One Needed to Know* for the Schoolwide Inc. Zing! digital library. This novel that has long languished in a forgotten file in my computer was given new life thanks to his great ideas and guidance. I'm ever hopeful the Zing! library, which is designed for teachers and schools to use on a subscription basis, will introduce Heidi and Donald to a lot of young readers.

Consider signing up for a Schoolwide Inc. subscription. There are many great books, including this one, available for readers from preschool through 8th grade. The books are divided into libraries according to reading skill level and subject matter, both fiction and nonfiction. It's pretty innovative. www.schoolwide.com/zing

When I was a kid, I didn't have any knowledge about Autism or have access to resources for siblings of Autistic children. I didn't even know the terms for the challenges with which my oldest brother struggled. I was simply told that he was 'slow'. In 1991 I began working as a teacher in Special Education and have been working with special needs students ever since. Years of training and experience has taught me a lot.

Thankfully, today there are many sources. If you'd like to learn more, here are some places to start.

https://www.autismspeaks.org/what-autism - a quick overview about Autism.

http://www.autism-society.org/living-with-autism/family-issues/siblings/ - some information and help for families with siblings of an autistic child.

https://ldaamerica.org/types-of-learning-disabilities/ - a website that explains a variety of learning disabilities.

http://www.helpguide.org/articles/abuse/dealing-with-bullying.htm - some advice for kids who are being bullied.

I know the r-word is used a lot in this novel. I'm sorry for that, but it was to emphasize how awful the word is. I hope you will take that to heart and refrain from ever using it as an insult or joke.
Spread the word to end the word: **http://www.r-word.org/**

"If we're going to make a real dent in the bullying issue, we're going to have to address the bullies themselves: find ways to help empower them that don't include allowing them to be predators or to simply be punished." Chris Crutcher, actor and children's book author

D. G. Driver is an award-winning author of Young Adult and Middle Grade fiction and member of SCBWI. Her other books include Purple Dragonfly Children's Book Award winner *Cry of the Sea*, *Whisper of the Woods*, *Echo of the Cliffs* and *Passing Notes*. She also has short fiction in a number of anthologies and some nonfiction published under the name Donna Getzinger. She lives near Nashville and is a teacher in an inclusive classroom of typically developing and special needs children in an Early Intervention program. When she's not writing or teaching, she might be found singing and acting in a local community theater musical with members of her talented family.

Learn more about her at: **www.dgdriver.com**

Follow her at
www.facebook.com/donnagdriver

www.twitter.com/DGDriverAuthor

www.instagram.com/d_g_driver#

CPSIA information can be obtained
at www.ICGtesting.com
Printed in the USA
LVOW11s0904190217
524726LV00003B/707/P

9 780692 829134